TOR

& THE NEIGHBOR

PAUL DUFFÉ

THE AUTHOR OF "TOR" AND "TOR & THE IMMORTALS"

BOOK

III

IN THE

TOR CAT
BOOK SERIES

Special thanks to Patrick Doran and Liz Flaisig for the editing services, Ryan Schinneller for the cover art and technical assistance, Tor, Poe, Buddy, O, Mazy, Holly, and my always faithful feline assistant, Studs.

Tor & The Neighbor

Prelude

Tor looked noticeably out of place sitting on the busy San Marco street corner. The San Marco community of Jacksonville, Florida, is a popular and trendy area located just outside the city's core on Jacksonville's Southside. Looking out across the busy intersection, Tor sat as still as an Egyptian statue. To the casual observer, he looked as if he was waiting for something.

Noticing a highly agitated man on the opposite side of the street walking down the sidewalk, frantically working with his cell phone, Tor stood up. In a sudden burst of speed, the cat raced diagonally across the intersection to the opposite corner. A red Mercedes coupe heading north on the right side of the road swerved to avoid hitting the animal, cutting in front of an oncoming city bus.

Reacting instantly, the bus driver swerved to avoid hitting the Mercedes. When he did, the bus crashed through a barrier city utility workers had erected around an open manhole. The bus's left front tire plunged into the open hole, violently jarring the bus and knocking the bus driver off his seat. Completely out of control, the bus headed straight for the man as he continued to fumble with his phone.

Hearing the out-of-control bus approach at the last

second, the man finally looked up, but it was too late. In a desperate attempt to stop the bus, the man put his hands out. The gesture was futile. The entire weight of the bus smashed into him, crushing him against a building. He was killed instantly.

From the opposite corner, Tor sat watching the carnage play out. Satisfied with the outcome, he casually trotted off and disappeared into a nearby neighborhood. Tor was on a mission only he could understand.

Chapter 1

A week after leaving San Marco, Tor arrived at his destination. He'd made his way to a small residential neighborhood about two miles south of San Marco. Casually walking down a quiet street, he heard voices and people splashing in a pool at one particular house. Recognizing the voices, Tor ran up the driveway and disappeared into a jungle of wildly overgrown vegetation straddling a chain-link fence separating two very different properties. The house of interest was to the left of the fence and laid out in such a way that it bordered a small, deep creek leading to the St. Johns River. The overgrown jungle along the fence had been left to grow wild on purpose for privacy.

Despite the neighborhood's close proximity to downtown Jacksonville, the large old-growth trees and dense vegetation gave the impression of being in a secluded wilderness sanctuary. Determined to get to the other side of the fence, Tor jumped to the top, but in the process snagged his collar on a sharp piece of broken metal fencing. Designed to break-away in just such a situation, Tor fought back, using his eighteen-pound body as leverage. Pulling back, he snapped the collar, freeing himself. Momentarily pivoting atop the fence, Tor listened to the voices. Again, hearing one that sounded familiar, he jumped to the ground. The broken collar fell off into the leaves next to the fence. Making his way through the dense underbrush, Tor found a comfortable spot out of the hot sun in the shadows where he could see people swimming and hanging out around a pool. Cautiously observing his new surroundings from the safety of his hidden vantage point, Tor appeared as if he was waiting for something.

Having been drawn to this particular house by instinct, Tor was content with laying low in the shade and taking in his new surroundings. Unseen in the bushes, Tor watched the lively group of young men and women as they horsed around in the backyard. The occasion appeared especially festive, and all were enjoying the party-like atmosphere. He could see one young man dancing to the music and waving a spatula in the air as he monitored the hamburgers and hotdogs he was cooking on a large grill. Several beautiful ladies were sunbathing and chatting excitedly on the pool deck while two other young men tossed a football between them as they floated on rafts in the pool. Tor immediately recognized the young men. These were the musicians who practiced in the rundown warehouse complex several blocks from Emma's home in Springfield. But he did not see the one particular young man he was looking for, not yet anyway.

Exiting from the kitchen through a large sliding glass door, Ryan Anderson emerged cradling as many beers as he could carry in his arms.

"Heads up!" Ryan called out as he tossed a beer to one of his buddies floating on a raft.

Seeing the beer flying toward him, Allen way overreached, causing his raft to slip out from under him. He just caught the bottle before crashing into the pool, creating a giant splash and completely disappearing beneath the churning waters. In a matter of seconds, Allen's hand appeared, holding the beer with his thumb over the opening. As he rose triumphantly from the water, he was greeted by lively applause from the others around the deck.

"Nice save," Ryan said.

After taking a long swig, Allen smiled wide. "It would be a shame to waste one of your fancy brews," he replied, victoriously holding the bottle up.

Shaking his head laughing, Ryan continued passing out the bottles of beer to his other guests.

"The good stuff, now this is more like it!" James said before making a toasting gesture in his direction.

"After last night, I thought we deserved it. That was the largest audience we've ever played for —and without a doubt, one of our best performances! I figured that was reason enough to share my 'good stuff' with the likes of you," Ryan said, raising his beer into the air. "To more nights like last night!" The others joined in, repeating the toast and hollering excitedly.

From Tor's vantage point, he could see everything. Recognizing Ryan, Tor stood up and stretched before venturing out from under the bushes and heading in his direction.

Just as Ryan finished his toast, Tor emerged into the yard. Seeing the cat in the distance, Ryan cocked his head, thinking it looked familiar, but he didn't have much time to ponder the thought. Feeling two powerful arms grab him around the torso, he had no time to react. James had run up from behind and forcefully tackled him into the pool.

As Tor exited the bushes, he stopped. Hearing a strange, muffled sound coming from somewhere in the neighbor's yard next door, he paused. The sound was familiar and reminded him of Poe. Listening for a second, he decided to investigate and returned to the underbrush in search of the mysterious sound.

When Ryan emerged from the frothing waters, he did not look happy. James immediately took off across the pool trying to get away, knowing Ryan would be looking to get some payback. But it was no use. Ryan's tight athletic physique, combined with years of competitive swimming, were no match for James. Within a microsecond, Ryan was on him like a shark attacking its prey. The others looked on laughing as James screamed before disappearing under the water. In a second, Ryan emerged holding something in his hand. Before James had time to chase him down, Ryan was already out of the pool.

"That's not right man, that's not right!" James protested, as the others laughed once they realized what Ryan had done.

"If you want them, you'll have to come get them," Ryan said, dropping James's swim trunks on the patio table.

James smirked and shook his head as the others taunted him.

"Okay, you asked for it," James said before walking through the shallow end of the pool and right up the steps with no hesitation. Standing on the pool deck, completely naked, he stretched before saying, "Seems a little breezy today."

The other guests started whistling and hooting and hollering loudly.

"Watch out ladies, James has unleashed the anaconda!" Allen joked.

"Now I see why you two have been together so long," one of the women said to the other.

Laughing, Ryan tossed the swim trunks to James and said, "Put that thing away before someone gets hurt." Everyone laughed. After suiting up, James bowed to a spontaneous round of applause and then jumped back into the pool.

Remembering the cat, Ryan looked out into the backyard, but it was gone.

Chapter 2

Entering the dense underbrush, Tor paused. Cocking his head, he again heard the strange, muffled sound. The vegetation growing between the two backyards was thick, but there was a well-worn trail at the base of the chain-link fence made by numerous animals on their way to the deep creek running behind the homes. Tor followed the trail, occasionally pausing to listen for the strange sound. When he reached a large oak tree straddling the property line, he found a gap in the fencing that made it easy to enter into the adjacent yard.

Unlike Ryan's well-manicured yard, the one next door was wildly overgrown. It was obvious at one point much care had been taken to create a beautiful landscape consisting of numerous flowerbeds, grassy areas, and impressive water features, but now it looked like an abandoned mess. Even the kidney-shaped swimming pool had been left unattended for some time. The stagnant water had turned a dark green color and was filled with leaves and other debris. Standing in the bushes, looking out into this sad landscape, Tor noticed a little girl sitting alone on a concrete bench holding a baseball glove. She had her head lowered and was crying softly.

Seven-year-old Cindy Collins often came to this spot to escape the tense atmosphere that existed inside her home. Little Cindy found comfort on the secluded bench hidden deep inside a heavily wooded corner of the long-neglected yard. After playing catch, she and her father would sit on the bench together and talk for hours. But after her father was killed by an unknown assailant over a year ago, Cindy had felt alone. Cindy's mother, Allison Collins, tried to the best of her abilities to comfort her daughter, but her own grief and the necessity of having to meet the new demands of the household presented her with many unexpected challenges. And her mother's new boyfriend wasn't helping the situation much either.

Randy Johnson, her mother's boyfriend, moved in about four months after Cindy lost her father. Randy was a former ex-boyfriend of Allison's. Their prior relationship was marked by many turbulent ups and downs. Randy had a violent temper that would often swing to the extreme. They were first together for two years until Allison finally had enough and started pushing him away. Randy had a hard time accepting this and for a while he stalked and harassed Allison, making her feel uncomfortable until she ultimately caved and let him back into her life. This cycle repeated frequently until she met Officer Mark Collins.

Mark was a five-year veteran with the Jacksonville Sheriff's Office when he and Allison first met. Being a police officer had always been his lifelong dream, and he'd served with distinction since joining the force. Mark and his partner at the time were familiar with Allison and Randy, having responded to numerous calls made by concerned neighbors when they heard Randy and Allison arguing. The visits ended peacefully enough, yet Mark and other responding officers always knew they'd be back.

But after one particular scary encounter where Randy's explosive temper got the better of him, Allison herself was forced to call the police. As fate would have it, Mark was one of the responding officers that evening. Allison had finally had enough. Mark was instrumental in helping Allison escape Randy and eventually get a restraining order against him. Concerned for her safety, Mark occasionally checked on Allison when in her area. At first, he kept their interaction very professional. But soon, his feelings became obvious, and they started dating. The more Mark was around, the less Randy harassed Allison. Before long, Randy was a distant memory.

Allison and Mark dated exclusively until she got pregnant. They immediately decided to get married and not long after found the perfect house and bought it. Mark liked to landscape and worked on the side as a landscape designer. He turned the exterior of their house into a beautiful oasis of serenity. He did such a good job that their neighbor, Ryan Anderson, hired him to design his backyard landscaping as well. Ryan and Mark immediately struck up a friendship and soon the three of them were the best of friends.

Not long after Mark and Allison renovated the house and property, Allison gave birth to their daughter, Cindy. Both could not have been happier. As the young family grew, Mark doted on Cindy to no end. They often spent many hours together in the yard and gardens. Cindy especially loved playing catch with her father. He gave her a baseball glove when she was very young, and they both shared a passion for the sport.

Unfortunately, the happiness the three shared was

not meant to last. On his way home one night at the end of his shift, Mark responded to a call about an intruder seen breaking into an abandoned residence. When he arrived on the scene and confronted the suspect, Mark was fatally shot. Allison broke down when notified of his death. She was so distraught, her parents had to temporarily move in to help run the house. Allison and Cindy were devastated.

Not long after Mark's funeral, Allison ran into Randy. He'd heard about what happened and offered his condolences. Maybe still grieving or just not wanting to be alone, Allison let her guard down where Randy was concerned and over time, allowed him to slowly reenter her life. It was casual at first, occasionally meeting for drinks and dinners. Randy was a familiar shoulder to lean on and ear to listen to her concerns. As the months passed, they got closer. He apologized for his past behavior and wanted her to know he was no longer the man he used to be. Allison believed him and soon they were together. It was sudden, but Allison was alone and scared for herself and Cindy. Randy appeared to be the perfect guy at the perfect time.

Everything changed shortly after Randy moved in with Allison and Cindy. At first, Randy helped take care of the landscaping and pool, his way of trying to convince Allison he really cared and wanted to help. But after he moved in, Randy's eagerness to help quickly evaporated. Everywhere he looked, he was reminded of Allison's former husband and the resentment began to build. Taking care of the house and yard irritated Randy. This was the man who took Allison away from him. The man she loved and had a child with. As time passed, he didn't just resent Mark, he hated everything that reminded him of Mark. Letting the landscaping grow wild was his way of killing Mark's memory. Within months, the house looked bad. Ryan offered to help, but this only further irritated Randy. He flew into a jealous rage whenever he would see Allison and Ryan talking. It got so bad, Allison found it easier to ignore Ryan all together. She even had to tell Cindy she could no longer hang out with Ryan after school since it upset Randy so much.

Within months of moving in, Randy had succeeded in cutting off most of Allison's and Mark's closest friends as well as turning her once-beautiful home into an unkempt mess. Any time Allison tried to tidy things up around the yard, Randy would fly into a rage, claiming she loved Mark more than him. It quickly became obvious that trying to convince Randy he was wrong was pointless. She found it easier to avoid the conflict rather than confront the reality of the situation head on.

Allison found an escape from Randy by working more. This was partly out of necessity. She did get some pension money from the Sheriff's Office after Mark's death, but she and Mark had leveraged everything they had to buy and renovate the house. They knew it was a risky move, but at the time they believed it was the right thing to do. Now, in order to keep the house, Allison found herself having to work more. It was important to Allison to keep Cindy in familiar surroundings. This was where she had memories of her father and where they all had spent so much quality time together as a young family. In Allison's mind, keeping the house was her way of trying to keep those happy memories alive for Cindy.

Unfortunately, Randy had once again succeeded in infiltrating Allison's life and was now meticulously trying to erase all traces of Mark. But the biggest reminder of Mark was Cindy herself. Every time Randy looked at her, he thought of the other man in Allison's life. At first, he tolerated Cindy because he had to. But as time passed, he became cruel and would often say hurtful things to her at every opportunity.

Cindy tried to avoid Randy as much as possible, preferring to keep to herself. Even though the gardens were wildly overgrown, Cindy would sit on the secluded bench and shut her eyes, thinking back to how things used to be. She'd remember playing catch with her father, helping him with the landscaping as well as how happy they all were playing and swimming in the pool with Ryan and their other friends. Recalling all the happy times made her feel good. But then she would open her eyes and be confronted with the harsh reality before her. Looking at the yard now, seeing the green pool and out-of-control vegetation made her cry. She sat on the bench depressed, lost in thought, longing for the past. Holding her glove, Cindy wept, remembering her father.

As Tor stood watching the little girl from a secluded position, he noticed a large snake emerge out of the dark creek water not far from where Cindy was sitting. Fortunately, this part of the creekbank was mostly dead grass and low weeds, so he could see clear down to the water's edge. It was a large water moccasin, one of the deadliest snakes in Florida. They were known to be very aggressive, and this one was heading straight toward Cindy. Tor quickly and cautiously crept down the edge of the brush line. He knew he didn't have much time, for the snake knew Cindy was there and was approaching fast. Cindy had her back to the snake, but her tiny legs were dangling from the bench. The snake had locked onto the movement and was positioning to attack. When it was within range, it stopped and coiled into a strike position. Just as it was about to spring forward, Tor leapt from the bushes and landed on the snake. In one powerful motion, he clamped his jaws around the snake's neck and held on. His eyes glowed brightly, drawing in the snake's lifeforce while at the same time crushing its neck and throat. Tor intended to kill this animal and had to be sure it was no longer a danger when he released it.

Hearing the commotion, Cindy jumped up and turned around. Tor had the snake by its neck and was violently rolling around on the ground as it fought back. It was a large snake, over 6 feet, but it was no match for Tor. After a minute or so, it was over. Tor dragged the snake a safe distance away from the bench before releasing his grip. Unlike other kills, Tor knew this one could still be dangerous.

The snake's body continued to twitch and move as its nerves slowly died. Soon it was motionless. Satisfying himself that the snake was no longer a danger, Tor walked over to Cindy who was looking on in amazement. Stopping a short distance away, he looked up at her and meowed lightly with a friendly greeting.

"Thank you so much Mr. Kitty! That's a water moccasin! My father told me they are very dangerous. Our dog, Biscuit, was killed by one last year. You saved my life! It could have killed me!" With that, little Cindy dropped to her knees and hugged Tor affectionately. Tor didn't resist. He let the little girl hold on to him. The friendly hug made him feel good and he started purring loudly.

Cindy released Tor and said, "Where did you come from? I haven't seen you around here before." She knew he couldn't answer, but she excitedly talked to him anyway.

"Are you hungry Mr. Kitty?" she asked, looking down at him. "I bet you are. Stay right here and I'll see what I can find for you to eat. It's the least I can do since you saved my life," she said, smiling wide and gently caressing his back.

Tor purred loudly and excitedly rubbed against her legs.

As Cindy started walking toward the house, Tor followed her. She abruptly stopped and whispered, "No! Mr. Kitty, you can't follow me. It's too dangerous. Randy better not see you. He doesn't like cats."

As if Tor understood her, he stopped and waited by a large overgrown bush. Cindy cautiously approached the back door leading to the kitchen. There were several ways to enter the house from the backyard, but this was the most direct to where Cindy wanted to go. Truth be told, she wanted to avoid walking through the house in order to avoid any contact with Randy.

Cindy slowly opened the door leading to the kitchen and quietly crept inside. Looking around, she could hear Randy in the den watching TV. He was laying on the couch. Occasionally Cindy could also hear Ryan's guests hollering and laughing as they horsed around in the pool. Randy could hear the commotion too and would shout out loud, "Shut the hell up over there!" Not that they could hear him. Still, it was obvious to Cindy that the lively atmosphere at Ryan's was irritating Randy. Cindy opened the refrigerator and retrieved some sandwich meat as well as a drumstick leftover from dinner the night before. She also got a small paper plate from the pantry. As quiet as a mouse, Cindy exited the kitchen the same way she entered.

After reaching the bench, she set the plate on the ground, then served Tor the sandwich meat and drumstick. Tor ravenously devoured both.

"Wow, you're a hungry cat. Enjoy it, you deserve it."

Tor finished his food, then laid on the bench next to Cindy listening to the little girl excitedly talk to him while coloring in one her favorite coloring books. Cindy had made the bushes and woods around the bench her own secret retreat, she called it her fort. She kept art supplies, coloring books, reading material and a variety of toys in a weatherproof chest her father had used to store cushions for the pool furniture. Feeling safe in her secluded corner of the yard, Cindy would entertain herself alone for hours until her mother came home from work. Even though Randy treated them both badly, he seemed to ease up on Cindy when her mother was in the house.

Tor laid on the bench watching the little girl play. Cindy was happy to have the company. It had been some time since she had anyone to play with, and the time passed quickly.

"Cindy honey, I'm home. Are you out here?" her mom called out from the pool deck.

Enjoying Tor's company, Cindy had completely lost track of the time. "My mom's home," she said, with noticeable excitement in her voice. "I have to go now." She called back and told her mom she was coming and would be there in a second.

Cindy quickly put her things back in the trunk. Turning to Tor she said, "Thank you again for saving my life. I wish I could bring you inside, but Randy isn't a very nice man. You'd be safer out here."

Hearing her mother calling again, Cindy hugged Tor tightly and again thanked him. "After school tomorrow I'll come out, and we can play some more if you want. Good night, Mr. Kitty, it was very nice meeting you" she said, hurrying up the path to her waiting mother.

From Tor's position, he watched as Cindy made her way through the tall grass and then ran to her mom and hugged her tightly.

"Good to see you too, lovebug. And what have you been up to today?" her mom asked, hugging her back.

Hesitant to say anything about the snake or cat for fear her mother wouldn't let her play outside anymore, she said, "Oh not much. Mostly I've been coloring and playing in my fort."

"That's nice honey." Her mom had to hold back a tear. She hated that Cindy couldn't play with her friends like she used to. But since Randy was home so often and didn't exercise any restraint when it came to his language around Cindy or her friends, they were not allowed to come over anymore. Also, many of Allison and Mark's former friends did not allow their children to play with Cindy in general. None liked Randy and made this clear to Allison. Although she hated this for Cindy, there wasn't much Allison could do about it. She knew Randy needed to go, but she didn't have the energy to confront him at this time. At the moment, Allison was doing all she could just to keep food on the table.

❧

After Cindy went inside with her mother, Tor returned to the path running along the fence and made his way back to the bushes where he'd been watching Ryan and his guests. It was starting to get dark, and the pool-party had long since broken up. The back of Ryan's house was mostly glass. From his vantage point under the bushes, Tor could see into the kitchen and living room with ease. He laid there watching the house for at least an hour. This had been his destination since leaving the Springfield neighborhood across the river a week earlier. But now he hesitated.

Ryan walked into the kitchen carrying a pizza that had just been delivered. A couple of Ryan's guests were still there and joined him in the kitchen as he set the pizza on a counter and then found plates and napkins for everyone. Tor watched the small group through the large picture windows as they interacted with each other. The atmosphere appeared lively. He could hear them laughing and almost shouting as they carried on over the pizza. Ryan appeared quite content interacting with his guests.

At this point, all Tor had to do was walk out from under the bushes and up to any one of the large sliding glass doors leading to the pool deck and he would be seen by Ryan, yet he hesitated. He continued laying there, stretched out like an Egyptian Sphinx, watching the jubilant group in Ryan's kitchen.

Suddenly he heard a crashing sound followed by irate shouting coming from Cindy's backyard. Tor quickly jumped up and ran down the path and through the opening in the fence. Cautiously making his way toward the commotion, Tor hesitated. Crouched down in the tall grass, he watched the scene playing out before him.

"If she doesn't want to eat her damn dinner, then tough shit! She had her chance," Randy shouted at Allison on the patio outside the kitchen. He had grabbed Cindy's dinner plate off the table, then walked out the kitchen door and forcefully threw it into an outside trashcan. The porcelain plate shattered into pieces, making a loud sound.

"Randy, calm down. She's just a child. She doesn't like brussels sprouts, she never has. I cooked them for you and me, not her. If she doesn't want them, it's fine," Allison pleaded.

"I'm sick of you always going out of your way to pander to her! She needs to learn she can't always get what she wants. You spoil her. Just like her father did. Well not anymore. It's time she realizes she can't have it her way all the time. You need to stop treating her like the spoiled little princess she thinks she is!" With that, Randy pushed passed her and went back inside.

Allison stood there biting her lip. She looked skyward, fighting the urge to cry. She missed Mark so much. Collecting herself, she went back inside to make Cindy another plate.

Tail twitching, Tor made a low-pitched growl as he watched Randy and Allison. He didn't like Randy. After meeting Cindy, Tor knew his mission had changed. Ryan would have to wait. Cindy was his priority now. Tor explored the neglected backyard and soon found a comfortable place to settle down for the night.

Chapter 3

Anxious and not able to sleep all night, Cindy was already up and mostly dressed when her mom knocked on her bedroom door to wake her up for school.

"Well, this is a pleasant surprise," her mom said, after finding Cindy almost fully dressed. She was just putting on her shoes when her mother entered the room.

"Good morning mommy," Cindy said, wide-eyed and full of energy.

Usually, it was a battle to get Cindy up in the morning. It wasn't that she didn't like going to school. On the contrary, she loved school —she loved doing anything that got her out of the house and away from Randy. The problem was, Cindy often had difficulty falling asleep at night. Though the house was spread out, nightly she could hear her mom and Randy arguing late into the evening. Worrying about her mom as well as missing her father, Cindy often laid awake listening to the commotion until she fell asleep from exhaustion. Truth be known, Cindy hadn't had a restful night's sleep since her father passed away. But this morning was different. Excited and ready to go, Cindy accompanied her mom to the kitchen and even helped her prepare breakfast. Little did her mother know, Cindy was on a mission of her own.

"And what gets you up so early?" Allison asked.

"I wanted to help you prepare breakfast this morning.

I was hoping we could make some bacon and sausage! I'm hungry."

Seeing the excitement on Cindy's face, her mom smiled and said, "Of course we can honey, but we'll have to be quick, we don't want you to be late for school." Allison knew she couldn't refuse Cindy's request. Seeing her so excited about something was a rarity these days. Even if it meant being a little late for school, Allison knew nothing was going to stop her from making breakfast with her daughter this morning.

With Cindy's help, Allison whipped up some scrambled eggs, bacon and sausage in no time. She also prepared enough for Randy so he would have something to eat when he got up later. Not working, he often slept until mid-morning most days. Allison was tired of fighting with him about finding a job. To her benefit, he was available to pick Cindy up after school and this saved her a small fortune by not having to pay for after-school care. Unfortunately, she had no idea what kind of environment Randy created for Cindy while she was at work. Cindy had stopped telling her mom how badly Randy treated her when she wasn't around because she figured her mother had enough to deal with herself when it came to Randy.

When her mom's back was turned, Cindy took some bacon and sausage from Randy's plate and quickly wrapped it in a napkin. Still unseen by her mother, she slipped it into her dress pocket before helping clear the table.

"Thanks mom, breakfast was good," Cindy said, placing her plate and juice glass on the sink counter while casually grabbing the key to the back door in the process. Using a small stepping stool to reach the upper lock, she then unlocked the kitchen door to go outside.

"Wait right there young lady. Just where do you think you're going?"

Not wanting to tell her mom about the cat, Cindy quickly came up with a reason. "I need to go to the fort to get some things for school."

"Ok, but be quick. You still need to brush your teeth."

Once outside, Cindy started quietly calling for the cat. "Here kitty, kitty, kitty."

Not seeing him anywhere, she made her way down the wooded path to her fort. "Here kitty, kitty," she quietly called again, but still saw no sign of the cat. Hoping he hadn't left the area, Cindy continued searching the backyard. Returning to the pool deck, she decided to search the other side of the yard as well.

Also heavily overgrown with weeds and small trees, this side of the yard had once been a beautiful rock garden peppered with large boulders and other impressive rock features. Knowing there were numerous places to hide if one was a cat, Cindy set about exploring the area in search of her new friend.

Again, Cindy called quietly, almost in a whisper this time. She made especially sure to keep her voice down since her mom and Randy's bedroom was on this end of the house. Her father had installed a set of French doors that opened to the garden. When the yard was kept up, the view from the bedroom was beautiful. But now, the curtains were always closed. Still, Cindy didn't want to wake Randy. Mornings were her and her mother's time together. Even though she knew Randy was in the house, she liked to pretend he wasn't around, and it was just her and her mom.

Hearing excited meowing coming from somewhere in the rocks, Cindy turned around to find Tor trotting toward her on the barely recognizable gravel path still winding through the neglected garden.

"There you are! I thought you left. I have something for you," Cindy said, pulling the napkin from her pocket. Tor was excited to see Cindy again. He rubbed against her legs and purred loudly.

Cindy giggled. His excitement made her feel good. It had been a long time since she laughed so freely. His display of affection meant so much to her. To Cindy, Tor was more than just a cat: he was a new friend.

She unfolded the napkin and placed it on the ground. Tor immediately devoured the contents.

"Wow! You're a hungry kitty," she said.

In no time Tor had eaten all the bacon and sausage. He then meowed and continued his excited purring and rubbing against Cindy. Still giggling, she sat down on a large boulder to pet him. "Ok Mr. Kitty, I have to go to school. You can stay here, but be careful. Don't let Randy see you. He doesn't like cats. If he sees you out here, he might try to hurt you, so stay hidden. When I get home, I'll find you and we can play together again at my fort."

"Hurry up honey, we're going to be late," Allison called

out the back door.

"Ok Mr. Kitty, I have to go. But remember what I said. Be careful and stay hidden. I'll see you when I get home from school." She hugged Tor tightly and then ran back to where her mom was standing.

"Did you find what you were looking for?" Allison asked, noticing Cindy came running with nothing in her hands.

"I couldn't find it, maybe it's in my room," she said.

"Well hurry up and brush your teeth. We need to get moving if we don't want to be late for school."

"Ok mommy," Cindy said, smiling big and running back to her room to brush her teeth.

Allison couldn't help but smile. It had been a long time since she'd seen Cindy so happy.

∽◦∾

Around 10:30a.m. that morning the bedroom French doors abruptly opened, and Randy stepped out. Wearing only his underwear, he stood on the threshold and stretched. At one point he had a fit athletic body, but now, his many months of inactivity allowed a noticeable pot belly and spare tire to form around his midsection. He yawned loudly and scratched his shaggy blond hair before stepping out onto the patio. He didn't go far. Standing on the edge of the deck, he pulled down his underwear and began urinating. He even made it a point to move around, spreading his piss as far as he could as if he was marking his territory. When he finished, he stood there for a second still exposed, then used both hands to shoot a bird toward the backyard. "Fuck you, you dead motherfucker," he said, before shaking out the last of the piss and pulling his underwear up. His contempt for Mark still burned red-hot. Weather permitting, this display of disrespect had become the morning routine most days. Exposing himself, pissing on the yard and then making a double "fuck you" gesture to Mark's work was Randy's way of getting back at Mark for taking Allison away from him all those years ago.

After relieving himself, Randy went back inside and slammed the French doors closed behind him.

Laying in a sunbeam concealed by thick vegetation, Tor's tail twitched as he watched Randy. Satisfied that he was gone, Tor stood up and stretched. He then casually strolled over to the area Randy had marked with his urine. Sniffing the air, Tor's nose twitched. He turned and backed to the edge of the deck, then sprayed the area down with his own scent. When he was finished, he kicked sand and dirt with his back feet over the area in a display of disgust, masking Randy's scent even more. Proud of what he'd done, Tor trotted off to explore his new surroundings while he waited for Cindy to come home from school.

Chapter 4

With Randy no longer contributing to the household finances, Allison was having a hard time making ends meet. The benefits she received after Mark's death had long since run out. Being the sole source of income for the household, Allison found it necessary to work more shifts and longer hours. As a certified nursing assistant at one of Jacksonville's largest hospitals, picking up the extra time was easy to do. If it wasn't for Cindy, Allison would work 24 hours a day. When Cindy was in school, she poured herself into her duties, doing anything to avoid being home with Randy.

Allison knew her relationship with Randy had changed. Maybe it was the fear of being alone or maybe it was his charm and the fact that he was there for her when she needed him after Mark was killed. Whatever it was, for a time when she was at her lowest, she found comfort in the arms of a man she thought wanted to help and be there for her in a time of need. But now, everything was different. Their relationship, for what it was, had changed. He had reverted back to the same jealous, possessive, overbearing and controlling man she remembered all those years ago when they were dating. Despite his claims that he had changed and was a different person, it didn't take long for the real Randy to reemerge.

Allison knew she had to end it with Randy. She knew he created an atmosphere of tension in the home. She hated exposing Cindy to his violent outbursts and explosive temper, and tried to shield her, but Allison knew she had to do more. She had to keep Cindy safe. She didn't feel Randy was a threat to them physically, but she knew his outbursts and behavior were not creating a healthy environment for Cindy.

Sitting on a park bench just a few blocks from the hospital where she worked, Allison was trying to grab a quick lunch. She liked this spot. The bench was under a large shady tree just off a popular walking path running along the edge of the St. Johns River. The river divided the city in half. At this particular part of the river, the view was beautiful. Allison looked forward to having her lunch there so she could enjoy the view as well as watch people strolling along the path. Despite the constant foot traffic, it was a great place to get away and enjoy some time to herself.

Sitting there watching the lazy river flow by, Allison remembered how happy Cindy was preparing breakfast with her that morning. Even being up and already dressed was a pleasant surprise. How could she refuse Cindy's request to help with breakfast? That look, and those huge, beautiful eyes melted her heart every time. She couldn't recall the last time Cindy was so excited. Realizing she was smiling, Allison lightly shook her head and quietly chuckled.

"Allison Collins? I thought that was you. Do you remember me, Daniel Baxter?"

"Daniel!" Alison recognized him immediately and practically jumped into his arms to give him a welcoming hug.

Caught off guard, Daniel was almost knocked down by the force of her embrace. Realizing she may have been a little too excited, she released Daniel as abruptly, again causing him to stumble. Both laughed as they pulled apart.

"I'm sorry Daniel, I didn't mean to throw myself on you like that," she said, trying to hide her embarrassment and regain composure.

"No need to apologize, it's not every day I get attacked by a beautiful woman," he said with a wink and a smile.

Allison pointed to the bench and asked if he would like to join her. He did. Daniel had been a big comfort to her after Mark was killed. He and Mark joined the police force at the same time, but Daniel had been more ambitious in pursuing his law enforcement career and was quickly climbing the ranks within the department. He had just made detective a year before Mark was killed. Though he was not investigating Mark's case at the time, he made it a point to check on Allison those first few months after Mark was gone. Daniel was married then and never crossed the line with anything inappropriate. He just wanted to make sure Allison and Cindy were coping as best they could.

The murder of a fellow officer had the department buzzing. Many volunteered their time to help in the investigation, but as the months passed, nothing new was discovered. This was tragic in itself, but also somewhat of an embarrassment. Not being able to find the killer of a fellow police officer did not sit well with many in the department. All believed Mark deserved better. Daniel took it upon himself to investigate the case, but couldn't devote as much time to it as he would have liked due to his own heavy caseload. Still, he made it a point to check on Allison and Cindy as often as possible.

After Randy entered Allison's life, things changed. He couldn't help but get the impression that Randy did not like him visiting Allison as often as he did. Not wanting to cause trouble for her, Daniel stopped coming around. Still, he always held a special place in his heart for Allison since he and Mark had been such good friends for so many years. Even as Daniel's and Mark's careers caused them to drift apart, they would occasionally run into each other at various police functions and when they did, it was like old times. Unfortunately, Daniel's wife, Connie, often did not join them due to a debilitating health condition, but she insisted he go and be with his friends as much as he could.

"It's so good to see you again, how's Connie?" Allison asked.

Lowering his head, Daniel became somber, "I'm afraid we lost Connie six months ago."

"Oh Daniel, I'm so sorry. I didn't know." She took his hand and squeezed it gently.

"So, how are you? How's Cindy?" Daniel asked, changing the subject. Then remembering Randy, he added, "Are you still seeing that guy, umm, Randy, was it?"

Allison's demeanor noticeably changed. Pulling her hand back, she turned away and fidgeted with her lunch container. "Yes, I'm still seeing Randy," she answered, nodding her head before turning back to face Daniel with a forced smile.

Daniel didn't need his detective instincts to know he'd hit on a sore subject. Even though she was doing her best to appear as she was just moments before, he could tell something had changed.

"And Cindy? How's she doing?" he asked.

Exhaling, Allison briefly hesitated before responding, "Cindy is still coping. She misses her father very much. The two of them had such a special bond," she said, fighting the urge to tear-up.

Reading the situation, Daniel put his arm around her and pulled her into him. That's all it took, the floodgates opened, and Allison began to cry.

"It's okay, Allison, let it out. I know this has been hard on you both. It'll be okay, I promise. It just takes time."

She calmed down, but remained in his arms. It felt good being held, letting someone comfort her and hold her for a change.

Then he asked, "And how are you?"

Daniel could feel her body tense before she slowly pulled away. Not facing him, she again shook her head and said, "I'm okay."

Daniel wasn't buying it. He got up and stood in front of her before squatting down to where they were looking each other in the eyes. "How are you really?" he asked.

She again started tearing up, so he rejoined her on the bench.

"It's okay Allison, you can talk to me, we're both survivors. If anybody would understand what it's like to lose the one you love, it would be us."

She slowly looked up to face him and wiped the tears from her eyes. "I'm not okay. I'm far from okay and neither is Cindy. I miss Mark so much —we both do." She looked at

Daniel through watery eyes, her lip quivering, her emotions overtaking her.

Daniel could feel her pain. He put his arm around her and pulled her into him. Both finding comfort in each other's embrace. Daniel held her tight. His eyes teared up as Allison cried on his shoulder.

Daniel could easily relate to what Allison was struggling with. After Connie passed away six months ago, he was a wreck. He and Connie had met in college and hit it off instantly. It was a true love story from the first day. After they graduated, they got married, deciding to face their future together. They supported each other in their careers as they set out to start their lives. Connie had always wanted to be a teacher, a noble profession and one she had the utmost respect for since teaching was in her blood. Her mother and grandmother were teachers, and Connie was determined to follow in their footsteps.

For as far back as Daniel could remember, he always wanted to be in law enforcement. He too was honoring a family tradition of sorts since both his uncles, and his father had been police officers. Daniel had great childhood memories of riding along with them in their patrol cars and getting to play junior police officer for the day. He fell in love with the idea of going into law enforcement at a very young age and never let anything get in the way of that dream.

After graduating college, he joined the police academy where he met Mark and the two became fast friends. Mark liked being a police officer, but Daniel's passion for the job far exceeded Mark's, allowing him to rise faster and farther than Mark in a relatively short period of time. Still, as Daniel's career advanced, he and Mark made it a point to stay close. For a while, Daniel, Connie, and Mark were like three peas in a pod. They did everything together. But as Daniel's career continued to take off, time and scheduling caused the trio to grow apart. By the time Mark met Allison, they were mostly just casual friends. Then, after Allison became pregnant with Cindy, Mark and Allison purchased a house and focused on starting their family together.

Daniel and Connie also attempted to start a family, but after several miscarriages they realized having children naturally might not be in the cards for them. Disappointed but not deterred, they began looking into adoption.

Working with small children all day, Connie loved the idea of being a mother and believed she would be great at it. Daniel, too, was excited about becoming a father and starting a family. Even though they were disappointed that they could not have children of their own, both were equally excited about the prospect of adopting a child in need of a loving home.

Unfortunately, just as the adoption process was getting underway and five years into her teaching career, Connie fell ill. It was quickly discovered that she had a rare form of leukemia. Immediately, they set out to get her all the necessary medical treatments, but it was to no avail. After a long and intense fight consisting of several bone marrow transplants and numerous other experimental efforts, Connie was exhausted. Accepting her fate, she made the difficult decision to stop fighting. Daniel was devastated. The thought of going forward in life without her was unbearable. But Connie insisted that this was what she wanted and that she was at peace with the decision. The truth was, she was simply tired of fighting and did not want to prolong the inevitable.

At first Daniel was mad. He felt Connie was giving up. But when Connie explained to him that she was suffering and wanted it to end, he understood. He was desperate to know what, if anything, he could do for her. Broken and emotionally devastated, Daniel kneeled by her bedside and sobbed uncontrollably, accepting her wishes. The only request she made regarding her care was to ask him to please be there with her in the end. It almost destroyed him, but he agreed and made it a point to be by her side until the final day.

Holding Allison tight, Daniel gently rocked her, aware a tear was rolling down his cheek. "It's ok Allison, let it out. I miss Connie every single day, too."

Allison slowly sat up and collected herself as much as she could. Noticing the tear on his cheek and his watery eyes, she tried to force a smile. "Thank you. I'm so sorry to hear about Connie. I feel bad for not knowing. It has to be just as hard for you, too. How do you do it? How do you survive each day and keep moving forward?" she asked.

Daniel looked down and then looked out over the river, as if he was remembering something only he could know before replying.

"Baby steps. At first, I needed to be alone, but eventually I poured myself back into my work. I used to be an intensely private person but now it's strange, I find comfort around my friends and coworkers more than not these days. Even to this day, I find it hard to be by myself for very long. We never had children so coming home to that empty house was hard at first, but over time, it got better."

Allison was quiet, reserved. The thought of a house without Randy actually sounded good.

"Fortunately, you have your daughter to help you get through. Connie and I were never fortunate enough to have children of our own. We were looking into adopting, but that never happened." He paused and looked down. "Oh," he said, remembering Randy. "And despite what anyone says, be happy that you have a new man in your life. That's good, Allison. I know you got a lot of heat and criticism for letting Randy into your life so soon after Mark passed. But just know, I understand. I understand because I know how hard it is to be alone."

Allison exhaled deeply and again shook her head as she turned away. "If only I could be alone," she uttered under her breath.

Noticing the abrupt change in body language, Daniel read the signs. So he asked, "Is everything okay with you and Randy?"

At a loss for words, Allison was momentarily speechless. Randy's sudden presence in her life was not taken well by many in her and Mark's social circles. Then, when Allison let Randy move in with her and Cindy so soon after Mark's passing, many of their friends were appalled. Allison quickly became the subject of harsh gossip, some believing she didn't love her husband, others even suggesting that Allison and Randy had been seeing each other behind Mark's back for some time and now she was free to see him openly. The trash talk became so bad that pretty much all their mutual friends cut Allison off, and those with children would not allow their children to play with Cindy anymore.

The truth of the matter was, in those early days and weeks following Mark's death, Allison was not herself. She was an emotional wreck, but managed to go through the motions as best she could. She was confused and vulnerable. Randy seized on this and used it to his advantage as he slowly began edging his way back into her life. They didn't even have sex until a month or so after he moved in.

Allison wasn't looking for someone to replace Mark, not at all. It was the loneliness, the physically being alone and the missing him that was so unbearable. She hated the uncertainty and just needed someone there to lean on and comfort her in that time of need. Randy made it a point to position himself perfectly at just the right time. Having a past with Allison and knowing her like he did, Randy was able to take advantage of the situation and play on Allison's vulnerability.

But as time passed, Allison realized letting Randy back into her life was a mistake, especially letting him move into the house. Yet every time she tried to correct that mistake, Randy would have an emotional breakdown, crying and even going so far as threatening to kill himself if she ever left him. The drama was too much for her to take, so she did nothing. Opting instead to choose the path of least resistance while trying to keep the peace and maintain some form of stability on the home front. She figured that was the best strategy at the time.

But now things had changed. Randy had changed. She knew she needed to get away, she just didn't know how. In that moment while talking to Daniel, her emotions erupted. She felt overwhelmingly trapped and frustrated. Almost as if someone took over her body and began speaking for her, she looked directly at Daniel and blurted out, "Randy isn't the guy he used to be, something's changed. I don't know what happened. Sometimes he can be such a nice guy then something triggers him, and he flies into a rage. At first, he was so loving and supportive. But then, not long after he moved in, he started becoming more and more angry. Small things would set him off. It's like he's always so resentful and mad. He constantly picks at Cindy and is so critical of everything she does. I know I need to leave him, and I've tried —several times– but he becomes so emotional, often threatening to kill himself if I go. It's so bizarre. He acts so unhappy when we're together and then, when I start talking about splitting up, he goes completely in the other direction. He says he would be nothing without me and couldn't go on alone. And for several days after a blowup everything is better, but then, inevitably, he returns to being the man he was. And now that he's injured and not working, I feel even worse about asking him to go without him having a way to support himself. But to be completely honest, I just don't have it in me right now to confront him. I'm just barely able to keep my head above water as it is. I feel so overwhelmed on all fronts and by day's end, I just don't have the physical energy for a confrontation. If only he'd go back to being who he was when he first came back into my life after Mark's passing."

"Back into your life?" Daniel asked. "You knew him

before you and Mark were together?"

Allison told Daniel about her first rather turbulent relationship with Randy. She even shared with him that Mark's handling of Randy was how they met. After Mark helped her escape Randy, the two of them fell in love and not long after started a life together. Daniel was not aware of their background. The more she told him about Randy and his prior behavior, the more he grew suspicious. Mark's murder was still unsolved and never sat well with Daniel or the department. Still, something always puzzled him about it. The nature of the killing was so brutal, almost executioner-like, a fact the investigating detectives decided not to make public or share with Allison. All she knew was that he had been shot responding to a possible suspicious person seen entering an abandoned house in a developing part of town. What she did not know was that Mark had been shot once in the stomach which brought him to his knees. It was surmised that the assailant then beat him across the face and kicked him multiple times before shooting him in the head.

Daniel knew the true facts, but the investigating officers kept the more unpleasant details to themselves; first to spare Allison the unnecessary heartache. But second, and more in relation to the case itself, they did it so that if they ever did catch the perpetrator, only the suspect would know the true details of the killing, offering even more proof that they had the right person in custody.

As Allison vented, Daniel listened intensely. Always the attentive detective, he was absorbing every word she said like a sponge. When she finished speaking, he took the opportunity to offer an opinion.

"I know it sounds harsh, but you have to look out for yourself and your daughter first. I'm sorry Allison, but as your friend, I really think you need to reconsider leaving him. The chances are he won't ever be the guy he was after Mark's passing. If anything, who he is now is probably closer to his true character," Daniel said.

Nodding her head in agreement, Allison said, "If only it was that easy. I still care about him Daniel, I do. But I'll admit, I think it was too soon for me to have gotten involved with anyone after Mark passed. I just don't have that kind of love for him and honestly, I never have. But yes, I hear you. I know what I need to do, it's just not the right time at the moment."

Having just run into Allison again after so long, Daniel didn't want to make her feel any more uncomfortable. He shook his head and said, "Well, if you ever need help with anything, just know, I'm always here for you."

"Thank you, Daniel, that means so much more to me than you know, especially now. And please know that I'm here for you, too. Sadly, we both share a painful and tragic experience." She reached out and squeezed his hand gently. "We both know what it's like to lose that special someone we love."

Daniel squeezed her hand back and nodded his head in agreement.

"Thank you, Allison. That means more to me than you know as well."

Noticing the time, Allison realized that she was already late getting back to work. After a hurried goodbye, she rushed back down the path toward the hospital. Fortunately, it was just a few minutes away.

As Daniel walked back to the car, his mind was racing. Not knowing about Randy all those years ago, he wanted to get back to his office and do some investigating. Something about Randy did not sit well with him and he was looking forward to finding out all he could about Randy Johnson and his past.

∽∾

When Daniel got back to the station, he immediately ran a background check on Randy. It didn't take long to find what he was looking for. He could see the restraining order issued against him by Allison all those years ago. He also saw numerous entries by Mark as well as other officers responding to domestic incidents corresponding to Allison and Randy's address at the time. Often calls were made by concerned neighbors. The responses were noted by the attending officers, but no action was taken other than making sure all parties were okay. This seemed to be the norm until one particular call; this one was noted as coming from Allison herself and it was followed by action. Randy was forcibly removed and taken to jail that evening. The arresting officer was Mark Collins.

"I'll be damned!" Daniel said, pushing back from his desk. He sat there tapping the chair arm with his fingers, in a state of disbelief. "Could it have been here all along and we just missed it?" As he searched Randy's arrest records, he noticed no other calls by Allison or the neighbors. As per what Allison had told him earlier that afternoon, he assumed this was probably because Mark was becoming a more frequent visitor in her life. He thought back to that time. Even though he and Mark had drifted apart as friends, he did remember when Allison came into Mark's life. All of a sudden, she was accompanying him to various police events. The two seemed joined at the hip and always together.

As Daniel continued to search Randy's background, he noticed numerous other complaints made against him from other women over the years, mostly domestic in nature. Allison was not the only one to have a restraining order issued against Randy, there were three others. As Daniel read on, he got a pretty good feeling that Randy might know more about Mark's murder than anyone knew.

Chapter 5

"About time! What takes you so long to get to the car every day? You know I do this as a favor to your mother. I don't have to be here. I have better things to do with my time than be your personal taxi," Randy snapped, when Cindy got in the car.

Randy hated picking Cindy up from school in the afternoons. He constantly complained about her being slow and having to deal with all the traffic when coming to get her. Fortunately, Cindy lived just a few miles from her school. If she was a little older, Allison would let her walk home with the other neighborhood children and their parents.

As much as Randy complained, this was the only thing he was currently doing that actually helped Allison. Since claiming to be injured on his former job, Randy wasn't working and did not appear to have any plans to find another job in the near future. Since he was available, Allison expected him to help with Cindy. It was the least he could do. The truth was, Randy picking Cindy up and getting her home also saved Allison a small fortune on after-school care. At first, Randy was more than happy to do it. But now, he acted like it was a huge inconvenience and complained constantly.

Cindy was used to the verbal assault; she got it daily. For her part, she would get in the back seat, put on her seatbelt and just stare out the window all the way home, not saying a word. Fortunately, the trip home was less than five minutes. But this was not the case for Randy. From the time she got in the car to them getting home, he would complain endlessly.

Still, this particular day, Randy's endless tirade fell on deaf ears. Cindy sat smiling to herself. She couldn't wait to get home; she'd been thinking about Mr. Kitty all day and was looking forward to spending time together in her fort.

As soon as Randy pulled the car into the driveway, Cindy's door flew open. She shot out of the car and was already inside the house before Randy was halfway up the sidewalk.

"What a stupid kid," Randy said, following her inside.

As was the routine, once they arrived home Randy would help himself to a beer, then go lay down on the couch in the den and watch TV until Allison got home to prepare dinner for them all.

Cindy typically put her school things away, changed, and then helped herself to an after-school snack her mom would leave in the refrigerator before either retreating to her room for the remainder of the afternoon or going to the fort and hanging out there until her mom came home in the evening. She tried to avoid Randy as much as possible because when they did interact, he treated her badly by saying cruel and hurtful things. She used to tell her mother, but over time stopped telling on him. After witnessing the many harsh exchanges between her mom and Randy, she worried her complaints would only make things worse.

Cindy also wasn't the typical seven-year-old. She knew her mom was hurting and missed her father terribly. She disliked Randy, but also knew her mother was afraid of him. Her mom had become trapped by his obsessiveness as well as their financial situation and Cindy was painfully aware of this.

Standing at the refrigerator, Cindy pulled out the snack plate her mom had left. Knowing Randy would help himself to the food, Allison hid other things around the kitchen that only she and Cindy knew existed. The plate in the refrigerator was the cut fruit and vegetables Cindy liked. Allison knew Randy wouldn't touch it since he hated fruits and veggies. Cindy took the plate and also prepared another small one for Tor consisting of sandwich meat and other random leftovers from the previous night's dinner. She then hurried out the back door to find Tor.

It didn't take long. As instructed, Tor had been waiting in the fort by the creek. When Cindy emerged into the small clearing, Tor hopped down off the bench and greeted her excitedly by rubbing against her small legs and purring loudly.

Cindy giggled at Tor's welcome. She prepared their snacks and then joined him sitting on the ground. Tor devoured the sandwich meat and other leftovers she had brought. Cindy, too, enjoyed her fruit and veggie snacks.

"Wow Mr. Kitty, you sure are hungry," she said, watching him eat. She gently stroked his smooth coat and occasionally petted him softly.

"Thank you for staying and being my friend. I don't have any friends since Randy moved in. He's not a very nice person.

The other kids around here are not allowed to come over when he's here." Cindy talked to Tor as if he was another child. To Tor's credit, he was very attentive and appeared as if he was listening to every word she was saying.

Time flew and the afternoon passed. After Cindy did her homework, she showed Tor all the toys she had hidden in her fort. She had a lively imagination and played continuously, often engaging Tor and bringing him into whatever she was doing. Tor engaged as much as he could, but mostly he sat on the bench and watched her play. At times, Cindy got the impression he was standing guard. Little did she know, she was right. Tor kept a watchful eye toward the creek, always looking for other dangers lurking there. But he also kept an eye out for Randy, too.

Chapter 6

The next day, Cindy anxiously sat at her school desk watching the clock. Usually, she couldn't care less that Wednesdays were half-days for her school. Other students looked forward to the shortened day knowing they were getting out early. Cindy dreaded early release. This only meant more time at home with Randy. But this Wednesday was different. Knowing she had a friend waiting in the backyard, she was impatient to get home. Finally, the last bell rang out. In a hurry to get in line, she grabbed her backpack and ran at full speed to the front doors of the school where the parents lined up outside to pick up their children. Surprised to see her, one of the teachers commented.

"Cindy! This is a surprise. I never see you here this early, you must have important plans this afternoon."

Cindy could not contain her excitement; a huge smile suddenly appeared on her face. Looking up at the teacher with big wide eyes, she nodded excitedly. "Yes, I want to get home so I can play with my new friend."

Automatically a smile appeared on the teacher's face. Cindy's story was known throughout the school. Knowing of her father's tragic loss as well as Randy's presence, made Cindy's situation the subject of conversation among the faculty. The teachers had observed a change in Cindy since her father's passing. She used to be such a lively little girl, always so full of energy and actively engaged with her classmates and in other school activities. But after losing her father, Cindy became withdrawn and preferred keeping to herself. It also didn't help that after Randy moved in, many of her friend's parents would not allow their children to go to Cindy's house if Randy was there. His language and bad temperament were not something they wanted their children exposed to.

And if this wasn't bad enough, Allison and Randy had become the subjects of vicious rumors and gossip between the parents. While many questioned the timing of Randy moving into Allison's house, others suggested that they had been having an affair behind Mark's back before he was killed. This talk was also known to the faculty. Despite the rumors and gossip, the school did its best to protect Cindy and tried to make her as happy as possible while she was in their care. In truth, the faculty felt sorry for Cindy and her mother.

Unfortunately, many of the staff were also very familiar with Randy since he was the one who often picked Cindy up after school. The routine was for the parents to wait in their car in a line outside the school and as each car approached, a teacher would ask them who they were there to pick up. The teacher would then notify another teacher who was in charge of overseeing the kids inside the school. When notified of which parent was there, the inside teacher would send the child out to meet their ride. More than a few times Randy's frustration at waiting was observed. If he wasn't unpleasant to the teacher, they often heard him scolding Cindy for taking so long to get to the car. Unknown to Randy, Cindy was never in a hurry to come out.

Seeing the excitement on Cindy's face, her enthusiasm

was contagious. Smiling, the teacher said, "That's great honey. I hope you and your little friend have a fun day."

When notified that Randy was waiting, Cindy shot out the front door and ran to the car.

"About time you got here, I wasn't going to wait all day," Randy barked, as Cindy buckled her seatbelt and settled into the backseat.

Fortunately, Cindy didn't have to endure Randy's verbal assaults for very long. When they reached the house, Cindy jumped out of the car and ran to the front porch. She was in such a hurry to get inside, she dropped her house key twice before finally unlocking the door. Eager to find Tor, Cindy went to her room and quickly changed into her after-school clothes before heading to the fort.

Randy exited the car, but hesitated. He leaned against the open driver's door and watched as Cindy ran inside the house. A twisted smile slowly began to take shape on his face. Satisfied Cindy was well into her routine, Randy closed the car door and then casually strolled up the sidewalk toward the house.

After getting home, Randy went to the den with a beer in hand and settled into his usual spot on the couch. As per her routine, Cindy snuck into the kitchen to retrieve the snack plate her mom had left. She also quickly made a plate for Tor, then quietly exited out the back door in search of her new friend.

When she reached the small clearing where the fort was, she called, "Kitty, Kitty, Kitty," but Tor did not appear. She called for him a few more times, but still saw no sign of the cat. She then made her way around to the other side of the yard where she had found him the previous morning and quietly called for him again, but still nothing. She knew she was home earlier than usual, so she figured he must be off somewhere. After all, there was no way for him to know she would be coming home early that day. A little disappointed, she made her way back to her fort where she planned to spend the rest of the day hanging out until he hopefully showed up later.

Watching from inside the house, Randy saw Cindy walking around the backyard, but could not hear her calling the cat. He briefly wondered what she was doing, but soon lost interest. Purposely standing back from the window so he wouldn't be seen, he watched as she disappeared down the path leading to her fort.

After Cindy returned to the fort, she went to the large weatherproof trunk to retrieve the items she would need for the afternoon. When she opened the lid, she immediately noticed the contents had been disturbed and one of the items she was looking for was missing. It was a pink plastic box about the size of a shoebox that contained all of her favorite crayons, colored pens, and markers. Searching through the contents of the trunk again, she still could not find it, it wasn't there. She searched the fort, but to no avail. She was certain she had returned it to the trunk the day before. She wondered if Randy might have taken it just to be mean. It wouldn't be the first time he'd done something like that. She walked to the edge of the creek thinking he might have thrown it into the water. When she reached the edge, she saw it. It was sitting on the end of their old dock. *How did it get out there?* she wondered.

The dock was dangerous. It was the only project in the backyard her father had not finished before his death. Mark warned her not to ever go out on the old dock for fear it might collapse. The wood was rotten and several of the support pilings were missing. Not much was holding it together these days.

Mark always dreamed of owning a boat, but after Cindy was born, that dream was put on the back burner. Many of the homes along the creek had small, short docks extending into the creek. Several of the homeowners were even able to keep some impressive boats tied up to their docks since they had the creek dredged to accommodate the larger vessels. Unfortunately, their dock was still in bad shape. One could reach the end if they were careful and walked along the far-right side, but to be safe, Mark did not want anyone on it until he made the necessary repairs.

When Cindy saw her box on the end of the dock, she knew it had to be Randy's doing. Not wanting to ask him to get it and knowing he would say no anyway, she decided to retrieve the box herself.

Cindy made her way through the tall weeds by following a path probably made by Randy earlier in the day. When she reached the old dock, she hesitated. Cindy remembered her father's warnings. She knew the dock was dangerous, but she was adamant about not asking Randy for help. Slowly, she made her way out onto the old, warped, gray wooden planks, carefully, stepping from plank to plank.

At first, the dock appeared solid, but as Cindy made her way farther out, she could feel it moving with every step. She tried to stay on the side her father said was good, but it still moved. Cindy was a little more than half way when she heard wood cracking. Freezing in place, she stayed calm. The box was only about ten feet away. Slowly, Cindy took another step. Again, she heard the cracking sound and froze in place. She knew Randy had to have been the one who put the box out there. She reasoned if it was strong enough to hold him, it had to be strong enough to hold her, so she took another step and then another. Staying as close as she could to the good side, she eventually made her way to the box.

When Cindy reached the box, she quickly picked it up and opened it. Satisfied all the contents were there, she closed it and started back. Slowly, she began retracing her steps the same way she had come. Again, Cindy stepped with caution. The cracking sounded louder on the way back. Then suddenly, out of nowhere, Randy's voice boomed out, "What are you doing out there?"

His shouting startled Cindy, causing her to lose her balance and misstep. Stumbling a little to the right, one of her small feet broke through a rotten plank, causing her to fall off the dock, splashing into the murky water below. Cindy could swim a little with her armbands, but without them, she panicked. Arms flailing wildly about, she desperately tried to keep herself afloat.

Watching from a higher point on the creek bank partly

concealed by brush, Randy just stood there. He looked on with no emotion as Cindy tried frantically to keep from going under.

Just then, Ryan Anderson emerged on his boat as it slowly made its way around a tight bend in the creek. He had been out on the river with clients enjoying the morning weather. Standing at the helm, he had to be cautious navigating the narrow waterway. The creek ran along the back property lines of about twenty homes before it exited into the river. It was a short creek and had several tight bends to contend with. Even though it had been dredged to a deeper depth for larger boats, it was still narrow and required some skill to maneuver around the tight turns. For Ryan's twenty-four-foot Monterey, it wasn't so bad. But other homeowners had considerably larger vessels that required an extreme amount of skill to navigate the narrow waterway.

As Ryan rounded the last bend leading to his house, he noticed Randy among the dense vegetation on the creek bank looking intensely at something. Following his gaze, it took him a second to fully take in the scene.

"Take the wheel!" Ryan ordered one of his passengers. Before the guy had time to reach the controls, Ryan had already dove over the edge of the boat and was speeding toward Cindy. All of his years of competitive swimming as well as the fact that he was in top physical condition, allowed him to move through the water at lightning speed.

"Cindy, are you here?" Allison called out as she walked in the front door of the house. Unknown to anyone, Allison decided to take a half-day herself so she could spend the afternoon with Cindy. Seeing how happy Cindy was the previous morning when they made breakfast together, she wanted to spend more quality time like that with her little girl.

Losing her father had been hard on Cindy, and Randy's change of behavior was not helping. After talking with Daniel, Allison knew she needed to do something about Randy. She knew his presence was not good for Cindy or her.

Those first many weeks after Mark's passing were a blur to Allison. From the moment she was told of his death, time stopped. Time literally stood still in her world. She remembered how the department stepped in to help with many details of the funeral service, as well as how her parents and other family members and even Daniel helped coordinate other aspects. She remembered being numb to all that was going on around her. Yet, somehow, she made it through. One day at a time.

After all the commotion began to settle, Allison, for the first time, realized she faced a future without Mark by her side. The thought of raising her daughter alone as well as trying to maintain the house was overwhelming. For days, she silently grieved behind closed doors, trying not to let Cindy see her crying. She knew Cindy missed her father terribly. She even, to some extent, found herself avoiding Cindy. Not because she didn't care about her, but more because she couldn't stand to look her in the eyes. It simply hurt too much seeing how badly she missed her father.

When Randy re-entered the picture and then offered to help, Allison was vulnerable. His intent seemed sincere enough and, in a way, she believed it might even be good for Cindy to have a male figure in her life. Not to replace her father, but as someone she could look up to and who could be there for her in a fatherly way. Unfortunately, as time passed, Randy proved not to be the man she hoped he would be. Allison knew it was time to do something about Randy and that was one of the reasons she came home early this day. She wanted to prepare Cindy for what she was finally ready to do, to leave Randy. Knowing how difficult it was leaving Randy all those years before, she wanted to prepare Cindy as best she could for what was possibly coming next.

But for the moment, Allison was determined to make the day about Cindy. She was looking forward to spending the remaining part of the afternoon with her daughter, enjoying some long overdue quality mother-daughter time together.

As Allison walked through the house, she was surprised she did not see Randy in his familiar spot on the couch in the den. Assuming Cindy was probably outside in her fort, Allison made her way to the kitchen to go out the back door. Passing through the den, she stopped. Looking out the wall of sliding glass doors, she noticed Randy standing in the bushes off the pool deck just above the creek. From her vantage point inside the house, she could clearly see him. He was just standing there, focused on something she could not see below him in the water. She wondered what he was looking at so intently. It almost appeared as if he was hiding in the dense vegetation. Strange, she thought to herself.

When Allison opened the kitchen door and stepped outside, she heard panicked splashing coming from the creek. She froze. Hearing a child calling for help, she recognized the voice instantly and knew it was Cindy. In a microsecond her motherly instincts kicked in, and she took off running down the path in the direction of the commotion.

Tor, being the curious cat that he was, had taken to exploring Ryan's backyard while Cindy was away at school. In stark contrast to Cindy's backyard, Ryan's was meticulously manicured. Having thoroughly explored Ryan's property during the day while Cindy was away at school and Ryan at work, Tor was very familiar with the layout. He was particularly fond of a certain lounge chair on a deck close to the creek. Curled up in the chair under the shade of a large tree growing over the creek and deck, Tor stretched, enjoying a gentle breeze.

Because his original intent was to find Ryan when he first arrived in the neighborhood a few days ago but was now focusing his attention on Cindy, Tor made it a point to explore Ryan's property when he was not around. Concealed in the bushes, Tor watched earlier in the morning as Ryan and his guests boarded his boat and departed for the day. Feeling confident he was safe and would not be discovered, Tor hopped up into his favorite chair where he comfortably waited for Cindy to get home from school. Unaware that Cindy was already home and that Wednesdays were half days, Tor remained stretched out in the chair enjoying the tranquility of his surroundings.

Lying on his back with his mostly white belly exposed, Tor was abruptly awakened by a loud splash and then panicked calls for help. Instantly awake, it only took him a second to realize it was Cindy's voice. He leaped from the chair and in a flash, shot across the yard toward the hidden opening in the fence.

⁋⁋

When Allison abruptly emerged from the path onto the creek bank, she briefly paused, taking in the sight. Ryan was speeding toward Cindy like a bullet in the water. All of his years of competitive swimming showed. Just as Cindy was about to go under, he grabbed her with one powerful motion by the back of her shirt collar, then swung her onto his back and told her to hold on. Wrapping her small arms around his neck, she did as instructed, still coughing up dirty creek water. Cindy knew she had been saved and felt a tremendous sense of relief as Ryan swam toward the shore.

Only hesitating long enough to take in the scene, Allison ran down the steep creek bank and right into the water to meet them as they approached. Ryan's passengers pulled the boat up just offshore and stopped as Ryan carried Cindy to dry land and gently placed her on the ground. She was coughing and scared but otherwise okay.

Allison dropped to the ground next to Ryan and Cindy. "Oh, my baby ... my precious baby, are you okay?" Allison repeated over and over as she held Cindy in her arms, rocking her, relieved.

Randy ran up joining them. "Is she ok? What were you doing out there Cindy? You know that dock is dangerous!" His tone was a mix of anger and concern.

Kneeling beside Allison, Ryan shot Randy a stern look that quickly quieted his inquiries.

Taking Ryan's hand, Allison reached out and asked, "How can I ever thank you?" She squeezed his hand and smiled while biting her lip, trying to hold back her emotions.

"No thanks necessary. I'm just glad I was at the right place at the right time," Ryan said as he stood up and locked eyes on Randy, who would not look at him. Ryan was suspicious. When they rounded the corner in his boat he noticed Randy on the creek bank. Ryan was sure he could see Cindy struggling and yet he remained frozen and partly concealed in the bushes. Something about the whole scene just didn't make sense.

Looking down at Cindy, Ryan pointed his finger at her. "And you, no more afternoon swims alone. If you feel like taking a dip, come get me next time." He mussed up her hair and gave her a playful wink and smile, then waded back into the water to join his friends on the boat.

"Thank you," Cindy said, waving as he climbed aboard. He waved back and then took the helm and slowly maneuvered the boat toward his dock next door. Noticing a pink plastic box on the console, he asked one of his guests what it was. The guest informed him that he fished it out of the water while they were waiting for him. Ryan opened the box and examined its contents. He quickly surmised that the box belonged to Cindy. Looking back toward the creek bank, he could just make out the three of them walking up the path toward the house before disappearing into the dense vegetation. When they unloaded the boat, Ryan grabbed the box so he could return it to Cindy at a more appropriate time.

ഇരു

Later that evening after Allison got Cindy cleaned up and in bed, she joined Randy in the den where he was stretched out on the couch watching TV. Allison took the remote and turned the television off.

"I was watching that," he said.

Allison ignored the obvious irritation in his tone. She stood with her arms crossed, partially concealed in the shadows facing him. "I saw you from inside the house today. You were just standing there on the creek bank. It almost looked like you were trying to hide in the brush. You were looking intently toward the creek. Just standing there looking. Why didn't you help? Why were you just standing there?"

She wasn't mad. Actually, she was unusually calm and expressed no noticeable tone. Instead, she was curious. She was confident in what she had seen. Seeing him just standing there, frozen. The scene was etched in her mind, and she was struggling to make sense of it. The image haunted her. Did he hate Cindy so much that he was willing to stand by and watch her drown? Her repeated cries for help could clearly be heard. Allison heard them and recognized her voice instantly when she walked out into the back yard. There had to be an explanation ...

Surprised by the question and even more surprised that she'd seen him, Randy sat up on the couch as his mind scrambled to come up with something.

"I was out in the yard and heard a loud splash. I was in the brush because I was trying to get a better look at what it was. I didn't hear any cries for help at first, just the splashing. Honestly, I didn't know it was Cindy. I was just trying to get a better look at what was making the sound. I thought it might have been a gator or something," he added, trying to be more convincing.

Allison remained motionless in the shadows, arms still crossed as what he said resonated. The silence was deafening. She had intended to confront Randy about him leaving when she got home, but after all the commotion, she didn't have the strength for all that that would entail. Instead, she nodded and tossed him the remote.

"It's been a long day, I think I'm going to bed. Don't stay up too late," she said, turning to leave the room. More confident now than ever, Allison knew what she needed to do. She heard his explanation, but didn't buy it. Still, it was late, and she was tired. Her confrontation would have to wait until the next day.

After she left the room, Randy's innocent facial expression eroded to a sinister scowl. "You were lucky this time Cindy, but next time Ryan Anderson won't be there to save your sorry little ass," he hissed, then focused his gaze back to a mindless TV program.

❦

Unknown to all, but after hearing the loud splash and then the frantic cries for help, Tor raced to the creek bank and remained hidden a safe distance away, observing the commotion. After Allison and Randy walked Cindy back to the house and went inside, Tor entered the clearing where her fort was. He sniffed the air until he caught a familiar scent, Randy's scent. He approached the cushion box and smelled it intensely. The scent was all over the lid of the box before leading out of the clearing and into the yard. He followed it. For Tor, scents were like colors. A fresh one was bold and easy to see and follow. But as it ages, it fades, losing its strength and becoming duller until it's so faint that it's no longer detectable. At this moment, Randy's scent was strong. He continued following it through the yard and down to the dock where it continued all the way to the end where Cindy's box had been placed. Standing on the end of the dock, Tor looked back at the house. His instincts were heightened; he sensed danger. Cindy was in danger. But to help her, he needed to be stronger, and there was only one way to find the kind of strength he would need.

Chapter 7

In the days following his arrival at Ryan's, Tor made himself at home in Cindy's overgrown backyard by feeding off lizards, frogs, and other wildlife living along the creek's edge, as well as enjoying the extra goodies Cindy brought him daily. The wildness of the property provided him with ample means to satisfy his natural predatory instincts. Rats and the occasional bird also brought some variety to the mix.

Still, Tor had a nomadic tendency. In the evenings, he started wandering farther into the neighborhood, exploring the surroundings. Days ago, when on his way to Ryan's, he passed a small strip mall with a seafood market located at one end. He remembered the location well and knew it wasn't far from Ryan's neighborhood. But what he especially remembered was the dumpster behind the market. He had spent a night there hunting. The dumpster proved attractive to many nightly opportunists looking for an easy meal.

As had become the evening routine and after Tor felt Cindy was safely asleep, he'd leave the neighborhood and go to the seafood market for some evening sport. The abundance of rats and mice helped satisfy an underlying craving only he could understand. At his normal pace, it usually took Tor about 30 minutes to get to the market.

This particular evening, just as Tor was rounding the corner of the seafood market on the way to the back alley where the dumpster was located, a car came racing down the road next to the building and abruptly stopped beside the dumpster. A highly agitated woman got out, mumbling to herself. She walked to the dumpster and quietly opened the large lid, being careful not to let it make noise. She then hurried back to her car where she retrieved a cardboard box about the size of a large toaster. She shook it hard then said, "I told him to take care of you and since he wouldn't do it, I will." With that, she threw the box into the dumpster, then quickly got back in her car and drove off.

After she sped away, the evening quiet was interrupted by ever-so-faint cries coming from the dumpster. Tor climbed to the top where the lid had been left open and looked inside. The box the woman had thrown in was laying atop the day's trash. Tor sat on the edge of the dumpster, examining it closely. Something inside was moving, causing the box to rock back and forth. High-pitched, frantic cries could be heard coming from inside the box. Tor moved closer.

The box had been loosely folded shut, almost as if the lady was in a hurry to close up whatever was inside. Using his paws, Tor was able to pull the folded cardboard flaps apart to reveal the contents. When Tor looked inside, he saw two small faces with huge, wide eyes looking back at him. One was a very small brown male tabby kitten, probably the runt of the litter based on its size. The other was a noticeably larger orange male tabby kitten. The smaller brown kitten started crying excitedly, determined to get out of the box to meet his rescuer. The other was quiet and more reserved.

Tor peered in at the two frightened little ones. There was

no hesitation as to what he needed to do. The bigger question was, how was he was going to do it? Two small kittens would be impossible to carry all the way back to the safety of Cindy's backyard. Both kittens were probably six or seven weeks old. Tor slowly lowered his head into the box and sniffed the two. The brown one eagerly tried to reach him by attempting to climb to the top of the box using his brother as a ladder. But the orange one was clearly frightened and remained frozen in the corner, eyes huge. Tor sniffed the brown one then turned to his brother. The little orange kitten hissed as Tor's large head approached. Tor paused, then his eyes started to glow a soft yellow-green. The glow was calming to the small orange kitten and soon he was more relaxed. Tor then used his mouth to gently pluck the smaller brown kitten from the box and carry him to the ground below the dumpster. Knowing the little one was vulnerable to other predators of the night, he raced back to grab his brother. When he got both kittens safely to the ground, Tor again gently used his mouth to pick up the brown one by the scruff of his neck. He turned to the other kitten and softly flashed his eyes at him again. As if directed to do so, the orange brother followed close behind Tor as they set off for the safety of Cindy's backyard.

The usual thirty minutes it took Tor to get back to Cindy's took a little over an hour this night. He took his time for the sake of the orange kitten's small legs. Even though he was about half again as big as his smaller brown brother, both were still small in stature. The distance was considerable for the little orange kitten, but he did a good job keeping up. It also helped that Tor was carrying the brown kitten in his mouth the whole distance, which slowed his usual more rapid pace. The only really dangerous part of their journey was crossing four lane San Jose Blvd. At most times during the day the road is packed with traffic, but at this late hour it was practically deserted. The three of them made it safely across the boulevard in one quick burst of speed.

When they finally arrived at Cindy's backyard, Tor brought them to a secluded cave he'd found days earlier in the neglected rock garden. It was relatively safe and well-hidden, thanks to the wildly overgrown vegetation. Tor instinctively knew the little ones were not out of danger yet. They were still vulnerable to a wide variety of predators, especially birds of prey and snakes. The secluded cave was the best he could do for the time being.

It was very late when they finally reached their destination. Tor and the orange kitten were exhausted, but not the little brown one. Having been carried the entire way, he still had energy to burn and was eager to explore his new surroundings. After repeated attempts to leave the cave, Tor finally laid across the opening to block his escape. Defeated, the brown kitten settled down and curled up next to his exhausted brother. It wasn't long before the three of them were sleeping soundly.

As had become the morning routine, Cindy got up early so she could sneak out of the house and spend time with Tor before school. She'd made it a point to raid the refrigerator first for anything she thought he might like, much to Randy's dismay. When she arrived at the fort that morning, she was met with a big surprise. Tor was sitting on the ground beside the bench licking his foot while the two kittens playfully wrestled with each other next to him.

"Mr. Kitty! Where did they come from?" Cindy's eyes were huge.

Hearing her voice, the two little ones ran behind Tor in an attempt to hide, but this was short-lived. Excited to see Cindy and to get the food he knew she'd brought, Tor walked to her, meowing cheerfully and rubbing against her legs. Completely exposed, the two little ones froze. They watched intently. Cindy was calm. She didn't want to frighten them, so she focused her attention on Tor and talked to him as she did every morning. It didn't take long for the brown one to get over his fear and follow after Tor on wobbly legs. Cindy spread the food out. Once the brown kitten realized there was food to be had, he excitedly pushed his way under and in-between Tor's legs to get to the food. Tor tolerated it because he knew the kitten was hungry. That's why he brought them to meet Cindy, he knew she'd be coming with the morning meal.

The orange kitten was still hesitant. He cautiously watched, his eyes huge.

Cindy softly talked to him while slowly placing some pieces of chicken on the ground. He crouched and lightly hissed, but then caught the scent of the food. Almost before Cindy retracted her hand, the little orange kitten was devouring the chicken. She smiled and repeated the gesture. When she went to give Tor more food, the orange kitten ran under and in-between Tor's legs to join his brother. Realizing she was going to need more food, Cindy excused herself and quietly snuck back into the house to find something else for the hungry group to eat.

After coming back and feeding them again, she sat on the bench with Tor. The brothers were wide awake and excitedly exploring their new surroundings in the early hours of the morning. Cindy and Tor sat watching the kittens like two proud parents until they heard her mother calling from the kitchen door.

"I have to go, Mr. Kitty. I need to eat my own breakfast before I go to school. Thank you for bringing your little friends. I hope they'll be here when I get home this afternoon," she said, and then hugged Tor excitedly. Hearing her mom call again, Cindy waved goodbye to Tor and the kittens before running back up the path.

Chapter 8

The school day passed with agonizing slowness for Cindy. All she could do was think about those two adorable little kittens. Finally, the last bell of the day rang, and Cindy wasted no time lining up to be dismissed.

"Well, this is a surprise," the line monitor said when she noticed Cindy standing in the front of the line again. Usually, she was one of the last students to leave.

Cindy smiled back with noticeably more enthusiasm.

Randy was surprised to be waved to the front of the line so soon. As much as he hated waiting, he'd become accustomed to Cindy being one of the last students out of the building.

"Why can't you do this every day?" Randy barked as Cindy opened the car door.

Cindy ignored him. Her mind had been on Tor and the kittens all day.

When Randy pulled up to the house, Cindy quickly jumped out of the car and raced up the driveway. Randy shook his head. "What a stupid kid," he said as he put the car in reverse and backed out of the driveway, still shaking his head.

It was Thursday, the only day of the week Randy looked forward to. This was pool night. Allison knew it wasn't worth arguing about and had long since relented. Truth be told, she actually looked forward to having him out of the house. With Randy gone, Allison made it a point to spend Thursday evenings with Cindy. Often, they'd prepare dinner together and then find a movie to watch. Usually both were fast asleep by the time Randy returned home.

Randy didn't have many talents, but he was good at pool. As a way to supplement his income, he used Thursday nights to hustle unsuspecting marks. To Randy's credit, by mid-evening he was usually flush with cash. Unfortunately, as the night progressed, so did his passion for drinking. Unknown to Randy, some of his marks were wise to his weakness. They even bought him drinks in the hopes of evening the odds in a rematch. By the time Randy made his way home, he typically had only about half of his winnings left. Still, it was enough to get him by for the week. As much as he detested working, he hated asking Allison for money even more. Pool was his way of supplementing his income and maintaining some level of independence.

Cindy wasted no time changing out of her school clothes and preparing something to take to Tor and the kittens. She quickly raced down the path to the fort, carrying what leftovers she could find. When she rounded the corner to the clearing, she immediately noticed Tor on the bench and the two kittens playing beneath him. Hearing her approach and spotting the plate of food, Tor stood and stretched. He then hopped down and excitedly greeted Cindy. The kittens were cautious, but once they realized Cindy had food, their fear fell away and immediately they were at her feet trying to climb her legs to get to the food. Cindy laughed watching them falling over each other as she prepared the plates.

After feeding her new little friends, Cindy sat on the creek bank playing with the kittens. Tor supervised approvingly from atop the bench. The kittens were particularly interested in a piece of string Cindy brought with her and were chasing it tirelessly all over as she played with them.

From Tor's elevated position on the bench, he noticed Ryan rounding the bend of the creek in his canoe. It wasn't uncommon for Ryan to take his canoe out on the creek after work. For him, it was a way to decompress and get a little exercise as well. Unseen by Cindy or the kittens, Tor quietly disappeared into the bushes but didn't go far, only far enough to conceal himself. Completely captivated by the kittens, Cindy didn't notice her neighbor quietly paddling up the creek in her direction. When he got close to the creek bank, he spoke out.

"Who are your little friends?" Ryan asked.

Surprised by his voice, Cindy spun around to face him. The kittens were also startled by the stranger and darted behind her.

When she looked at Ryan her face registered fear, almost as if she'd been caught doing something wrong.

Ryan sensed this, so he calmly sat in the canoe with the paddle laying across his lap. His smile was warm, and that always made Cindy feel comfortable.

"They just showed up this morning. Please don't tell my

mom or Randy," she pleaded. "I know Randy would make me get rid of them."

Ryan raised his hand to his mouth and made the gesture of locking his mouth with a key then throwing it into the creek. Then a huge smile to affirm his commitment.

Noticeably relieved, Cindy smiled back and thanked Ryan. The gesture was so sweet it almost brought a tear to his eye.

Noticing the kittens hiding, Cindy dangled the string in front of them. "It's ok little ones, Ryan's a friend," she said, coaxing them back into play mode by wiggling the string. It took no time at all for the kittens to bounce back to full speed. Watching the duo chasing the string made for great entertainment. Ryan and Cindy laughed while they played.

As he watched Cindy play with the kittens, Ryan was aware of a constant smile on his face. It had been a long time since he'd heard her laugh and seen her smile so freely. Prior to her father's passing, Cindy was such a lively child. He'd often hear her giggling and playing with her parents and friends in their backyard. Ryan was no stranger to their home nor them to his. Many weekends they'd all go out on his boat and spend the day on the river together.

After Mark's death, Ryan helped where he could but when Randy came into Allison's life, it was obvious he wasn't comfortable with Ryan hanging around, so it wasn't long before their friendship drifted apart. Ryan was aware of Randy's jealous nature and had overheard many heated exchanges between Allison and Randy after he would see them talking from time to time in the driveway. It also didn't help that Ryan was very physically fit and often ran and exercised outside shirtless. Allison had long since become desensitized to Ryan's physical presence and never paid it much attention, but not Randy. He'd get enraged when he saw her talking to Ryan without his shirt and accused her of being unfaithful and more. Over time, it was just easier for Allison and Cindy to avoid Ryan all together. Ryan had an instant dislike for Randy, but tried to hide it for Allison's and Cindy's sake. Still, he missed hanging out with them and especially missed the sound of Cindy's laughter.

"So, what are you going to name them?" Ryan asked.

"Well, I'm not sure. I've been calling the orange one O, and his little brother, Buddy."

"Works for me. Keep it simple," Ryan said, nodding his head in agreement.

Noticing the plates and respecting the fact she wanted to keep the kittens a secret, Ryan asked, "So how are you set for food?"

Frowning, Cindy shrugged her shoulders. "I've been sneaking them things from the refrigerator."

Ryan again smiled. He knew two small growing kittens would need more than that, so he pretended to think.

"Humm. I'm thinking these guys are going to need more food as they grow. How about I go to the store later and get you a bag of kitten food. You can hide it here in your fort."

Cindy's eyes lit up. She was so excited. She would have given him a huge hug if he wasn't floating in the canoe. "Thank you so much! I promise I'll pay you back from money

I've saved in my piggy bank," she said. Her excitement touched Ryan deeply.

"No need. I'm your co-conspirator, so it's my pleasure. I'll head home so I can go to the store. I'll leave it here on the creek bank in a little while. Just be sure to put it in that storage box before night falls so other animals don't get into it."

Cindy was so excited. Her enthusiasm was contagious. It warmed Ryan's heart to see her this excited about something. Within the hour, Ryan used his canoe to paddle back over with two bags of kitten food so he wouldn't be seen from the house, unaware Randy was out for the evening. He wasn't surprised to find Cindy still playing with the kittens. Cindy happily took the bags of food and placed them inside the large box for safekeeping.

"Oh, and don't forget this," Ryan said as he reached under the seat of the canoe and pulled out her pink plastic box.

Cindy's eyes lit up. "Where did you find it? I thought it was gone forever!" she said, taking it from him.

"One of my guests recovered it while I recovered you," he joked.

"Thank you so much! My father gave me this box," she said, hugging it against her chest, noticeably relieved.

Ryan had to avert his eyes. The moment was so innocent and sweet it made him tear-up. Focusing on the dilapidated old dock, a thought occurred to him.

"Cindy, can I ask why you were out on that dangerous old dock?"

Cindy became somber as she looked at the ground,

avoiding his gaze.

"Hey, it's me, I'm already your partner in kitten crime," Ryan joked, trying to lighten the situation. He noticed a slight smile appear on her face after saying that.

"Well ..." She hesitated for a few seconds. "I had to go out there to get my box," she answered pointing to the end of the dock.

"Your box? That box?" Ryan asked, confused.

Cindy nodded her head but remained quiet.

"What was your box doing on the end of the dock?"

Again, not looking at him, she just shrugged.

"Who put your box on the end of the dock?" Ryan asked with growing concern in his voice.

Again, she just shrugged.

Remembering seeing Randy on the creek bank, Ryan asked, "Do you think it was Randy who put it out there?"

Again, Cindy shrugged. Then added "Maybe ..."

Ryan's heart skipped a beat, but he remained calm. Seeing that asshole on the creek bank made more sense now. He was watching. He must have seen the whole thing. Did he intend for that to happen? Was he intentionally trying to hurt her? Alarmed, he knew he needed to talk to Allison, but for the moment he'd be calm.

"Cindy, as your friend, I need to ask you a question and please be honest with me. Will you be honest with me?"

She again nodded.

"Has Randy ever hurt you or your mom?"

She shook her head no then looked up at Ryan. "But he does yell a lot, and he breaks things. He gets really mad at me and mommy all the time."

Ryan felt his temperature rising, but remained calm. He never liked Randy. He could tell Cindy was getting uncomfortable with their conversation, so he didn't ask any more questions. He did ask to borrow a pen and a piece of paper from her box. He used the pen to write down his phone number on the paper and then gave them back to her.

"If you or your mommy ever need me, just call. I'll be right over. Okay?"

She looked at the phone number and smiled. "Thank you, Ryan. You're a good friend."

He winked at her and said his goodbyes. As Ryan paddled back to his dock, he couldn't shake an uneasy feeling that something bad was about to happen ...

Chapter 9

The next morning, Detective Daniel Baxter was parked inconspicuously down the street several houses away from Allison's home. From his vantage point, he watched Allison and Cindy load into her car and then pull out of the driveway. Allison usually dropped Cindy off at school on her way to work and counted on Randy to pick her up in the afternoons. She would prefer Randy get a job, but for the time being his unemployment did help her save money by not having to pay for afterschool care.

Daniel chuckled to himself when noticing the time. It was 7:30a.m. He figured Randy was still fast asleep. The idea was to catch Randy off guard. In his experience, he found people are usually not at their best when surprised, especially early in the morning. After running into Allison and reviewing the casefile, Daniel was eager for a confrontation with Randy. He still might not be their guy, but he sure checked all the boxes for being a person of interest. How Randy was overlooked by previous investigators still puzzled Daniel. He figured so much was going on at the time that somehow Randy must have fallen through the cracks. But after talking with Allison and learning about their prior relationship and the circumstances under which she and Mark met, he felt Randy was definitely worth a second look. Opening the car door, Daniel couldn't help but smile when he stood to put on his coat. Looking both ways before crossing the street, he started whistling a happy-go-lucky melody as he made his way toward the house to confront Randy.

ॐॐ

Allison had wanted to talk to Cindy about leaving Randy when she came home from work early Wednesday afternoon, but because of the creek incident, she decided to hold off. It had already been a trying day, and she was exhausted. She knew when she did confront Randy it would require all of her strength and energy. Having dealt with him in the past, Allison knew what she could be in for, which was why she wanted to talk with Cindy first and prepare her for what might happen.

Allison exited the neighborhood and instead of heading toward Cindy's school, she turned the car in the opposite direction.

"Mommy, you're going the wrong way," Cindy said, wide-eyed, looking at her mom and pointing out the window.

"I know honey, I thought we would go by the donut shop first and have some donuts. I also want to talk to you about a few things."

She had Cindy at the word donut.

After going through the drive-through, Allison pulled the car over under a large oak tree and parked. She sipped her coffee while Cindy enjoyed her donut and hot chocolate. Cindy looked up at her mom smiling from ear to ear, her mouth smeared with pink icing from her favorite strawberry donut with sprinkles. Laughing, Allison took a napkin and cleaned the mess off her face. "Looks like you're wearing more of that donut than you got in your mouth."

After cleaning Cindy up, Allison sat back in her seat and looked at her in that admiring way a mother looks at her child. It so warmed her heart to see Cindy smiling and enjoying herself. She knew the last year had been hard on her. Cindy loved her father so much. She even felt a certain amount of guilt for not being there for her as much as she knew she should have been. In those early weeks and months after Mark's death, Allison poured herself into her work to avoid coming home. Not because she didn't love her daughter, but because Cindy reminded her so much of Mark and the life they once had. She knew it wasn't fair to Cindy, but at times, the feelings so overwhelmed her she barely had time to get away before she was overcome by emotion.

Allison also knew Randy had not helped the situation. Randy clearly was a mistake, and she knew it. She knew it at the time. She had hoped he would be good for Cindy. Never to replace her father, but instead more like someone to help fill that void as a friend. Unfortunately, that did not turn out to be the case. Randy losing his job and not making any real attempt to find another one put more responsibility on Allison to support the household. Randy did help save on the cost of daycare, yet that hardly offset his own expenses.

Even more troubling was how Randy treated Cindy. At first, they got along well. Randy helped maintain the yard and spent quality time with them both. But after he moved in, he started changing, becoming more agitated by the house, the yard upkeep, and especially Cindy. He felt she was spoiled and that her father had let her get away with too much. He felt she needed more discipline. He never hit her, but would often yell and cuss at her. He would even take her toys away and sometimes break them on purpose. Cindy was a constant source of contention between Allison and Randy. They would frequently fight late into the night about her. Unfortunately, little did Allison know, Cindy could hear the arguments from her room. Nightly, Cindy cried herself to sleep worrying about her mom.

Allison hated herself for letting things go as far as they did. She had no real excuse other than the fear of confronting Randy and the fear of being alone. But after the creek incident the previous day, Allison knew what needed to be done. Almost losing Cindy jolted her awake. She'd already lost one person she loved; she wasn't going to lose her daughter, too – and she especially wasn't going to let Randy intimidate either of them any longer. She didn't buy his excuse that he couldn't see what was going on in the water. Something about the way he was standing there just didn't sit right with her. She didn't want to believe it, but it almost looked as if he was hiding in the bushes on purpose. Did he hate Cindy so much that he wanted her dead? The thought was so disturbing she quickly put it out of her mind. Instead, she focused on the task before her. Taking a deep breath, Allison took Cindy's little hand and gently squeezed it. "Honey, I need to talk with you about something because I want you to be prepared," Allison said, patting her hand and looking at her with a reassuring smile.

Cindy's expression became serious. She looked so small sitting in the passenger seat, but at the same time there was a maturity about her, too. Not a common trait in the typical 7-year-old. No, this maturity had been shaped and forged through the tragedy and trials of the past year. This was the maturity of someone who had endured so much and yet still found the strength to get up each morning and face the day with renewed hope. This was the well-earned maturity of a true survivor.

"Yes mommy, what's the matter?"

Her soft, innocent voice melted Allison's heart. "I just wanted to say I'm so sorry for everything over this past year. I wasn't there for you as I should have been after we lost your daddy. And I'm sorry about Randy and how he treats you," she said, nervously rubbing Cindy's hand. Allison's lips quivered and her eyes filled with tears as the emotions began to overwhelm her. "I'm sorry—," she started, but was abruptly cut off by Cindy reaching up and wrapping her mom in a smothering hug. At that point Allison could no longer control the flow of tears. She hugged her little girl back, sobbing uncontrollably. They held each other in a loving embrace, both comforting and grieving. For the first time since Mark's death, both cried on each other's shoulders, both there for the other, both understanding the depth of pain and feeling of loss each shared.

Allison told Cindy what her intentions were for Randy and tried to prepare her for what to expect. She knew Cindy was strong, but she also knew Randy. She hated having to do it, but she refreshed Cindy on how to call 911 in the event of an emergency.

Cindy listened intently as her mom explained about her and Randy's past relationship and how her father was instrumental in helping her get away from Randy at that time.

When Allison finished, she sat quietly. Cindy reached over and took her mom's hand.

"It will all be okay Mommy; everything will be okay."

When Allison looked at her, Cindy's warm smile filled her with the reassurance and confidence she needed.

"Oh honey, I love you so much," she said again, hugging her tightly.

Allison held Cindy in her arms, gently rocking her, then slowly pulled back and said, "Ok, how about we make one more trip through the drive-through and then get you to school."

Cindy's eyes lit up, and she bounced excitedly in her seat, knowing another strawberry donut with sprinkles was in her future.

❧

After Allison dropped Cindy off at school, she decided to head home and confront Randy. Knowing how difficult he was most likely going to be, she figured it would be better to do it now while Cindy was in school. Just as she started pulling out of the school parking lot her phone rang. It was the hospital. She was late and hadn't called in so they were concerned. They were also extremely shorthanded due to some unexpected scheduling mix-ups and were trying to pull in all the available personnel they could find. Allison knew she needed to confront Randy and get it over with while Cindy was safe at school, but it was also Friday. Maybe she could arrange for Cindy to stay with her sister over the weekend and do it then.

Allison was clearly conflicted and disappointed. Unlike other times when she would have welcomed an excuse to avoid dealing with Randy, this time was different. This time she was ready. But Cindy ... Cindy had already been through so much. It wasn't fair to expose her to the abuse she was sure Randy would throw at her. No. This time she was putting Cindy first. She decided she would call her sister when she took a break later in her shift and see if she could arrange a sleepover for Cindy, so she'd be out of the house when she confronted Randy. As Allison pulled her car forward toward the school parking lot exit, she again hesitated before turning in the direction of the hospital. Clearly disappointed, she sighed.

"This ends tomorrow no matter what," she said out loud, then accelerated toward the hospital.

Chapter 10

Standing on Allison's front porch, Daniel straightened his jacket before ringing the doorbell. The early morning quiet was only interrupted by the singing of lively birds as they were waking up to greet the day. He listened intently, but heard no activity from inside the home, so he rang the bell again, this time also knocking loudly on the front door with his fist. Within seconds there was an unmistakable response from inside the house. Chuckling, Daniel stepped back a little on the porch when he heard highly agitated grumbling growing louder as the voice approached the door.

Daniel was already prepared, holding his badge, ready to display it to the irritated occupant. Just for good measure, he rang the bell again.

The front door suddenly swung open to reveal a disheveled, sloppily dressed and clearly irritated Randy.

"What the hell do you want?" Randy barked.

Daniel remained calm. "Good morning, I'm Detective Daniel Baxter from the Jacksonville Sheriff's Office, is Allison Collins home? I'd like to speak with her please." At the same time, he presented his badge.

Randy's surprise was obvious. He wasn't afraid of the police, quite the contrary. If anything, he despised them. Still, he knew it was in his best interest to cooperate or at least appear to do so.

"She's not here right now. She just left to take her daughter to school and then she's going to work. What do you need to talk with her about?" Randy's tone was a mix of curiosity and disgust. He had no respect for law enforcement, but he was also curious as to why a detective wanted to see Allison.

"And you are?" Daniel asked, already knowing full well.

"Randy Johnson, I live with her."

"Oh, that's right. She mentioned you when we spoke," Daniel casually commented. He wanted Randy to know that they had already talked, he hoped it would rattle him, not knowing what was said.

"Well since you're home, do you mind answering a few questions?"

"What is this about?" Randy demanded.

Daniel could sense Randy had little respect for law enforcement, so he changed his strategy.

"We've come across some new information in the murder of Officer Mark Collins, Allison's former husband. And because of this new information, we're reviewing the case, looking for anything we might have missed. Basically, we're backtracking and giving the case a fresh new look-over." Daniel let what he said sink in before continuing.

"So, tell me Mr. Johnson, how long have you and Mrs. Collins known each other?" He already knew the answer.

Randy nodded, but did not invite Daniel inside. He was clearly caught by surprise and briefly stalled as he came up with a response. For a split second, he wondered what this new information was that they had, but he kept his composure and remained calm. Then his whole demeanor changed before answering, "I've known Allison for a while. I moved in here a few months after Mark was killed to help out with things."

Daniel's eyebrows instinctually raised, but before he could ask the next question Randy volunteered more information.

"We got together a little while later and have been together since."

Daniel assumed by his crude reference that he was referring to them having sex. "So, it's safe to say you and Mrs. Collins are more than friends these days?"

Randy nodded in agreement, but gave no verbal response.

"Did you know Officer Collins, her husband?"

Randy's irritation was obvious as he shifted his weight from one leg to the other. "I didn't know him personally, but I knew of him. He and Allison were together before me."

"So, you're saying you had never met him before the two of you started living together?"

Randy stood there silent. He felt the detective was fishing, but he wasn't sure what for. "Yes, that's right. I'd never met the guy."

"Now that's interesting. You see, we've been reviewing old case reports that Mark filed years ago pertaining to certain domestic disturbances and your name came up more than a few times. It appears you and Allison had a history before she started seeing Mark. There were numerous reports of the police being called about her boyfriend at the time. It seems Mark showed up on at least three of those occasions and confronted the boyfriend. He even helped Allison get a restraining order against the guy. Does any of this ring a bell?" Daniel asked. His expression was ice cold, no emotion.

Randy remained silent, but he looked as if daggers might shoot from his eyes at any second. Daniel was a little surprised by his reaction. Randy didn't look scared or intimidated, instead he had a cocky arrogance about him.

"Maybe I did meet him a few times back then, so what? Allison and I were going through some things, and we had a lot of problems at that time, but we worked it out and are together now."

"Well, that's good to hear. Still, I have to ask, you know, for the record. Can you account for your whereabouts the night Officer Collins was murdered?" Daniel knew that was a bold question, but he wanted to ask it anyway. He was curious about the answer.

Randy's posture became more rigid. He stepped forward in an attempt to intimidate Daniel, but his flabby belly hanging out from under his soiled tank top only made the gesture comical. "I can't say that I remember where I was or what I was doing that night," Randy said, stepping to within a few inches of his face. It was clear he hadn't showered. His pungent body odor engulfed Daniel in a sickening cloud.

Daniel locked his eyes on Randy's and held the gaze. Then a sly smile slowly emerged on his lips. "I'm sorry to hear that." He took a small step back and reached into his coat pocket to retrieve his card. "Here, please give this to Mrs.

Collins when she gets home and ask her to call me. I have more questions I'd like to ask her."

Randy took the card.

Daniel nodded and thanked Randy for his time and then strolled back to his car. If he had any doubts as to Randy's guilt, they were gone. He was eager to get back to the station and continue working on the case.

Randy remained standing on the porch and watched as Daniel drove away. He rolled the card between his fingers then looked at it one more time before flicking it into the overgrown bushes next to the porch and walking back inside the house.

୧୭

After Daniel left Randy, he went to the station and again reviewed Mark's case file. The shooting seemed so personal. It was determined that Mark was first shot in the stomach which brought him to his knees. The coroner then believed he was pistol-whipped and kicked a few times before he was shot in the head. These details were never made public and there was no need to share this information with Allison or anyone else for that matter. The investigators decided to keep these facts to themselves in the hopes of being able to have it validated by the perpetrator when finally caught.

Unfortunately, an unexpected change of leadership in the investigation occurred a few months into the original investigation. The lead detective on Mark's case resigned from the force unexpectedly due to a family emergency.

The case was then passed to Detective Steven Bronson, a respected yet heavily over-loaded member of the department. Still, this victim was a fellow brother of the shield, so Detective Bronson did his best to make the case a priority. He, along with numerous other law enforcement personnel, volunteered countless hours of their personal time to canvas the neighborhood, looking for the discarded weapon as well as talking to numerous residents in the hopes that someone might have something of importance to contribute. Over and over detectives and other officers returned to the neighborhood to see if anyone had learned of any additional information that might prove helpful, but every time they were disappointed. Rewards were even offered, but nothing of significance was ever discovered. It was as if the killer had simply disappeared into thin air without a trace. The perfect crime.

Daniel reviewed the case notes and saw where one of the previous investigators suggested the possibly of a random encounter with an unknown homeless person who might have been using the abandoned home as shelter. Noticing that the previous detective noted that the house was abandoned got Daniel's attention. He was curious about the location and wanted more information about the home and how it was that Mark just happened to be there that night.

Looking through the case notes, Daniel saw where Mark responded to the call about a suspicious person being seen entering the residence in question at 11:45p.m. The neighborhood was a mix of older homes and new construction. Various developers had bought properties in the area and were in the process of rehabbing them. The neighborhood was old and part of a historical district, which meant the homes and structures were protected and could not be torn down without the permission of the Historical Society. This particular area was also proving popular with younger couples because of its charm and location near a thriving downtown entertainment district. Many developers were trying to cash in on the area by buying homes and property in the surrounding neighborhoods in an effort to renovate and flip these properties for a healthy return. Unfortunately, not everyone was successful. Because of the age of the homes and buildings, as well as the strict historical requirements, not all would-be investors profited. The particular home where Mark was killed had been abandoned several weeks earlier when the developer ran out of money. His company had to cease work on several other nearby projects as well as lay off personnel.

Daniel knew Randy worked in the construction trade and was curious if he had worked on or around any of the projects in the area. Another question to ask Randy the next time they met, he noted.

Still, something was eating at him about the location. Daniel pushed away from his desk and leaned back in the chair, hands clasped behind his head, lost in thought. Is it possible Randy lured Mark to the abandoned house to kill him? Had Mark's murder been premeditated? And if so, why then? Why wait six years to finally kill the guy? What was the trigger that set him off six years later? Daniel's mind raced trying to find a motive, but nothing obvious stood out. Still, he was certain Randy was their man. After the encounter earlier that morning, he felt confident of that. The bigger challenge now was how to link Randy to Mark's murder –and prove it.

Daniel looked up at a picture hanging on the wall. It was his police academy class graduation picture. He pushed himself up from the chair and walked over to it. Looking at himself and Mark standing together, he shook his head. "Don't worry buddy, I'm on this. I'll get the prick who killed you if it's the last thing I ever do," he said out loud, lightly touching the frame of the picture and then exiting the office. Daniel knew that many of the people who originally worked on the case were still around, so he set out to interview anyone he could find who might have more information about Mark's shooting.

Chapter 11

Unfortunately, the staffing situation at the hospital did not improve as the day went on and Allison ended up having to stay the entire shift since they were so shorthanded. She'd hoped to get off work in time to pick Cindy up from school, but the shortage prevented her from leaving early. She knew Cindy would be disappointed when Randy showed up, but she reasoned this would be the last time. Allison also called her sister to arrange a weekend sleepover for Cindy, but to her dismay, was informed that her sister was currently out of town and would not be back until the following week. She was hoping to have Cindy out of the house when she talked with Randy, but now that didn't appear to be a possibility.

Still, Allison was ready to confront Randy. All day she'd been thinking about what she was going to say and how she would do it. She knew from past experience that it was bound to get ugly, but she was determined, even if she had to call the police. Seeing Randy standing on the creek bank still did not sit right with her. The way he was standing there just didn't make sense. He even looked like he was enjoying what he was watching. *Did he really dislike Cindy so much that he wanted her dead?* As hard as Allison tried to push the thought out of her mind, it kept creeping back in. That image of Randy standing in the bushes haunted her.

Sitting in the breakroom lost in thought, Allison was interrupted by her supervisor.

"There you are. I've been looking all over for you. Cindy's school called, apparently nobody came to pick her up and she's still waiting."

Allison called Randy, but got no answer. She tried calling him a few more times, then told her supervisor she had to leave to pick Cindy up.

As Allison drove to Cindy's school, she briefly entertained thoughts that maybe something had happened to Randy. *Maybe he left her or had been in a fatal accident.* She knew those were horrible thoughts to have, yet, in the back of her mind, she was hopeful something had happened that would rid them of Randy for good. But the more likely explanation was that he had gotten drunk and passed out or was off with his friends partying somewhere. Still, there was no denying that Allison was relieved Randy was not picking Cindy up today. For the first time since Randy moved in, she didn't feel comfortable with him around Cindy. All the more reason to get on with the confrontation she was determined to have.

Cindy was sitting at her desk happily drawing in the aftercare classroom when Allison walked into the room. The fact that Randy had not picked her up and that her mom was coming to get her, had her in a good spirits.

"I'm sorry baby, I've had a crazy day at work."

They briefly hugged, then Allison helped Cindy pack up her belongings. As Cindy was packing her backpack, Allison noticed the picture she had been working on laying on the desk. The drawing was of three cats all sitting together. One was a clearly larger black and white cat sitting next to two smaller kittens, one orange and one brown. Allison was impressed by the detail in the drawing. She picked it up and said, "Wow baby, this is really good."

Turning back and realizing her mom was holding the drawing of Mr. Kitty and the kittens, a sly smile appeared on Cindy's face. "They're my friends," she said, taking the drawing and gently packing it in the book bag with the rest of her belongings.

Allison sensed there was a deeper meaning behind the drawing and briefly thought about getting a kitten for Cindy once Randy was out of the picture.

On the way home, Allison told Cindy that she had not yet spoken to Randy but planned on doing it the next day. She also told her she would have preferred for Cindy to be out of the house while she spoke with him, but it didn't look like that would be possible.

Cindy was disappointed to find out Randy was still at the house. When Randy had not picked her up from school, she hoped it was because he was gone. Unfortunately, that was not the case. Still, seeing her mom and hearing her reassurances filled her with optimism that soon things would be better for the both of them.

When Allison pulled into the driveway, she was surprised to see Randy's car missing. Again, she momentarily wondered if something really did happen to him.

As they were getting out of the car, Ryan pulled into his driveway next door. Seeing Ryan, Cindy enthusiastically shouted hello. Hearing her, Ryan returned her enthusiastic greeting with one of his own. Cindy then turned and ran to the front door and let herself inside the house.

"She seems to be in a good mood today," Ryan said to Allison, while gathering some items from his car.

Allison smiled as she watched Cindy run into the house. "Yes, she does, doesn't she?"

Instinctively looking to see if Randy was around, Allison called Ryan's name and walked closer toward him. There was a low, thin hedge separating their driveways which created a small three-foot barrier between the two. Allison looked a little humbled and smiled nervously, unsure of how to start the conversation.

Ryan could tell she had something on her mind. "Is everything okay?" he asked, noticing her hesitation.

Allison looked at him and forced another smile. "I'm going to ask Randy to leave this weekend," she said, nervously looking down and picking leaves from a branch on the hedge.

Ryan nodded his head in agreement and said, "I think it's for the best."

There was no sympathy or effort to question the decision on his part. Allison was momentarily shocked by the bluntness of his response, but it quickly passed. She understood how Ryan felt and why. To keep the peace in her own home, she had sacrificed their friendship over the past year.

Allison bit her lip, forcing a fractured smile. Ryan could see she was doing all she could to keep herself together, so he smiled reassuringly. "I think you're doing the right thing for yourself and Cindy." He hesitated for a second then added, "Especially after what happened in the creek."

Allison's look said it all. "You don't think it was an accident either, do you?" she asked.

Ryan took a deep breath and then exhaled. "Something just doesn't add up. When we came around the bend on the boat, I could see Randy in the bushes. To me, it looked as if he was just standing there watching Cindy struggle in the water. But honestly, I didn't have a lot of time to analyze it."

"He told me he couldn't see what was in the water." She paused, then looked directly at him. "I went out there this morning and stood where I thought I saw him standing and I could clearly see the spot where you rescued her."

Both were silent for a moment before Ryan continued. "Well, since we're being honest, I think you should know I talked to Cindy the next day. I asked her why she was out on the dock. She told me she went out there to retrieve her pink drawing box. She said somehow it had found its way out to the end of the dock."

Allison's face registered shock. She didn't want to believe Randy could harm Cindy but now, knowing this, her suspicions were confirmed. "Oh, dear God, is it possible he really did want to hurt her? I know he can sometimes be cruel, but he hasn't ever done anything physical —to either of us."

Ryan shook his head in disbelief. "I don't know, but like I said, something just doesn't add up."

Again, both stood in silence as the substance of the conversation sank in. Then slowly, Allison nodded her head with growing confidence, knowing what she needed to do. She wiped a lone tear from her cheek before brushing the hair off her face. She smiled and looked at Ryan. "I'm going to confront Randy when he comes home. Can Cindy stay with you this evening while I talk to him? I was hoping to get her to my sister's this weekend, but that's not possible."

Without hesitation Ryan agreed. He informed Allison that James, one of his bandmates, was coming over soon to pick up some equipment and work on the playlist for Saturday night's performance, but he would be happy to have Cindy over. Allison was relieved. She knew how Randy could get and didn't want Cindy experiencing any part of what might happen. She also knew there was a very real possibility she might have to call the police if things got too far out of hand. They talked a little longer about the band and their recent surge in popularity. Allison remembered James and asked Ryan to say hello for her. Back when Mark was alive, she and Mark often came to their performances when Ryan and the band first started touring. Ryan jokingly referred to Allison and Mark as his most loyal groupies.

Ryan met his bandmates completely by accident one night when he was singing along with some friends at a bar. The band had just been forced to dismiss their lead singer right before a scheduled recording session. Two of the band members wrote songs for a living and sold them to other performers. Often, they'd record a series of demos to offer as samples. They were just about to head into the studio to start recording their latest round of demos when their lead singer crashed hard. He'd been struggling with addiction for years. It seemed the more pressure he was under, the more he abused.

Finally, they had to cut him loose. Defeated, two of the band members decided to drown their sorrows at a local bar where they ran into Ryan and his friends. The rest was history. After more drinks and some serious coaxing, Ryan agreed to help them with their recordings. James, the self-proclaimed leader of the band, even convinced Ryan to perform live and he was hooked. Something about performing in front of live audiences was like a drug to Ryan and soon he and the band were becoming popular regulars on the local music scene.

Ryan never intended to go into the music business. On the contrary, he was very successful in his advertising career and from the beginning made it clear to James and his fellow bandmates that that was his main priority. Still, as the band's popularity grew, Ryan knew he might one day be forced to make a choice between the two. But for now, he was fortunate to have both options in his life, and he was eager to make the most of each while he could.

Ryan informed Allison that he would be home the rest of the night and to send Cindy over when she was ready, they'd listen out for her. Allison's relief at having a safe place for Cindy was obvious. After saying their goodbyes, Ryan watched Allison slowly walk back toward the house. He knew she was determined, but he could also tell she was scared, so he called her name. When Allison turned around Ryan said, "If you need anything don't hesitate to call or come over. I'll be right here if you need help with anything —anything," he stressed a second time. Ryan didn't like Randy and wasn't afraid of confronting him. If anything, he looked forward to having the opportunity to finally kick his ass.

Allison smiled back. She had a renewed look of confidence about her. "Thank you, Ryan. I really appreciate that," she said, then continued on to the house.

Cindy wasted no time changing out of her school clothes and was already at her fort playing with the kittens by the time her mom came inside the house. Allison opened the back door and thought about calling Cindy in so she could get her ready to go Ryan's, but as she stood holding the door open, she could hear Cindy giggling. It sounded like she was happy, so she decided to let her play while she showered and changed out of her work clothes.

Tor waited with the kittens for Cindy to arrive and dispense the food. Happy to see her, he enthusiastically rubbed against her small legs while purring loudly. He took a few bites of food and then left Cindy to play with the kittens. In a way, Tor was relieved to have Cindy home. During the day he'd become a babysitter of sorts for the kittens. Since they were so small, he knew dangers lurked everywhere. Snakes, birds of prey, and even Randy's occasional ventures into the yard to relieve himself could all prove deadly to the curious little ones. While Cindy played with the boys, Tor casually distanced himself from the group by exploring the creek bank farther into the yard and overgrown brush. He was driven to satisfy a craving only he could understand.

Chapter 12

As Randy drove back to Allison's house, that all too familiar feeling of bitter resentment began to grow. He hated even looking at the house. Seeing it, the yard, and especially Cindy, always reminded him of Mark. The man Allison left him for —the man who, in his mind, took her away from him. For a while, when he first moved in, he got a sick satisfaction out of living there. In his own twisted way, Randy reasoned that he'd won. Mark was gone and he was back in Allison's life. But as time passed, his victory began feeling more like a prison. Everywhere he looked, he was surrounded by reminders of Mark. The house, the landscaping, everything had Mark's touch on it. As much as he tried to neglect the yard and house, Randy still couldn't escape the fact he was living in the remnants of another man's life, and he hated it.

When Randy first moved in with Allison and Cindy, the landscaping was beautiful. But soon, his resentment began to show. In an effort to erase Mark's presence, Randy started neglecting his duties around the house. Conveniently, he claimed his most recent work injury not only prevented him from finding another job, but also from doing any of the landscaping tasks he so eagerly agreed to do only months before. Since Allison could not afford to hire anyone to take care of the property, she started doing much of the yardwork herself, but even this irritated Randy. He became jealous and angry when she'd spend time in the yard. To Randy, it was as if Allison was cheating on him with Mark. Spending time in the yard was spending time with Mark, and this made him furious. Over time, Allison figured it was better to avoid encouraging such episodes, so she avoided doing work outside unless it was absolutely necessary. As needed, Allison would mow the front lawn to appease the neighbors, but even this occasionally caused problems.

Randy would have preferred they move to another house, but in order to worm his way back into Allison's life, he originally sold himself as eager to help with the household responsibilities and caring for Cindy. Little did Randy know, but Allison's financial situation was not as solid as he originally assumed, and it wasn't long before the reality of their circumstances set in. Allison could not afford to move. If anything, she was doing all she could just to keep her head above water. Randy soon realized he'd trapped himself in a role he had no real intention of playing long-term and became resentful. Neglecting and abusing the house and yard was his way of fighting back against Mark's memory. The house had become a prison of his own making.

When Randy reached the house, he noticed Allison's car in the driveway.

"Shit!" he said, banging his hands on the steering wheel. "I forgot to pick the brat up from school."

Occasionally, Randy would forget to pick Cindy up. This usually happened when he got his days confused. Not working, he sometimes lost track of what day of the week it was. But that wasn't the cause this day. Officer Baxter's early morning visit did more than just interrupt his typical routine of sleeping the day away. After the encounter, Randy was irritated and could not go back to bed. He paced the house for hours, wondering what Allison and the detective had already talked about. *When did they talk and why didn't she say anything to him about them reopening the investigation?* he wondered. The more he thought about it, the angrier he became. *Another police officer butting into his personal life was unacceptable!*

Remembering back to his first relationship with Allison, Randy recalled when Mark first entered the picture. On several occasions, other tenants in their apartment complex would get so concerned about Randy's explosive temper that they called the police when they heard Randy and Allison arguing. In response to one of these calls, Mark and his partner encountered Allison and Randy for the first time. After arriving at their apartment, the officers paired off with each of them to discuss the situation one-on-one. It was clear even then that Randy didn't like seeing Allison talking with Mark. He was handsome, with a 6'2" frame that revealed he was a man who took care of himself. Randy watched as Mark and Allison talked. Mark had an infectious smile. His sandy blond hair and blue eyes radiated a sense of warmth and calm. Allison was clearly at ease in his presence and seemed as if she was enjoying their conversation. Randy was fixated on the two of them so much, that the officer addressing him had to constantly redirect Randy's attention to his questions. Randy's obsessive fixation was so obvious, it was even noted in the officer's report. Fortunately, on that occasion there had been no physical assaults committed and both parties seemed to want to work it out. After a half-hour with the two of them, the officers left. But both officers had a strong feeling that this would not be the last time they or their fellow officers would be visiting this address.

A month later, the officer's concerns were proven right. This time Allison herself called the police. When she arrived home after work Randy was acting erratically, and Allison feared for her safety. Ever since their encounter with Mark and his partner, Randy had been accusing Allison of having feelings for Mark. Working as sporadically as he was, Randy often spent much of the day sitting in the apartment, letting his imagination work him into a jealous rage. Some days when Allison would return home after a long day of work, Randy would begin accusing her of sneaking around and seeing her police-officer boyfriend behind his back.

But this last encounter was particularly disturbing. Randy had worked himself into a state. When Allison arrived home, he was already hostile and had been drinking heavily. He began accusing Allison of wanting to see other men. Randy became belligerent and destructive and even broke furniture in an attempt to frighten and intimidate her. Scared, Allison locked herself in the bedroom and called the police. Mark happened to be on duty that night and again he and his partner responded to the call. When they arrived, Randy was drunk and out of control. He even attempted to take a swing at Mark, which immediately got him arrested. They took Randy to jail, mostly to sober up.

After his shift, Mark stopped by Allison's apartment to check on her. The visit was sincere and conveniently on his way home. After what unfolded the previous evening, Mark wanted to make sure she was okay. Allison greeted him warmly and confided in him that she wanted to leave Randy, but was fearful. She wasn't sure how to do it and asked if Mark could help. Having seen many such instances, Mark was surprised by Allison's determination. It had been his experience that the partner who called the police often felt guilty and allowed the abuser back into the home. But not Allison. In Mark's opinion, this separation had been long in coming. It also helped that Allison had a place to stay once she left the apartment.

When Randy was released from jail later that afternoon, he came home to find Mark and his partner there. Even though they were technically off duty, they promised Allison they would be there for support. When she told Randy she was leaving, he again became irate, but this time he was sober and better able to control his temper. With the two police officers standing by, Randy said nothing as Allison gathered her clothes and personal items before being escorted to her car. They then followed her to her sister's house, where she was going to live until she figured things out.

Unfortunately, Randy knew where she went and began driving by and stalking her. He was determined to get her back. The more she refused, the angrier and more unstable he became. When his efforts proved unsuccessful, he vandalized her car and started leaving threatening voicemails and texts. Desperate for help, Allison again reached out to Mark. Knowing the law was limited in what protection it could provide from a jealous ex, Mark encouraged her to get a restraining order. With Mark and his partner at Allison's side, the judge wasted no time granting her request. After Randy was served the restraining order, his harassment drastically diminished. Though relieved, for months Allison lived in constant fear Randy would retaliate in some way.

Fortunately, over the following weeks, Mark continued to check on Allison, and this did much to help restore her confidence. As the visits grew more frequent, it became obvious Mark and Allison looked forward to seeing each other and soon they became a couple. Some people thought they were moving too fast, but to Allison and Mark, they felt as though they'd known each other forever. Both were the love of each other's life. They shared a peace and comfort that they'd never known before, a true inner connection that they never knew they were looking for but had finally found together. The perfect true love. It wasn't long before Allison moved into Mark's apartment.

Randy was well aware of Allison and Mark's relationship. Despite the restraining order, Randy stalked Allison for months. He was jealous of Mark and resented his involvement in their lives. Eventually, his fixation on Allison began to diminish, but it was never really extinguished. For years he occasionally watched her from afar even after she and Mark bought the house and started building a life together. All the while his resentment and jealously continued to simmer. In Randy's mind, Mark had taken Allison away from him. It wasn't so much about love, but possession, property. Allison was his and Mark took her from him. As the years passed, Randy's obsession with Allison ebbed and flowed as he entered into new relationships of his own. But when his relationships would ultimately end, he always found himself back spying on Allison from afar.

For years, it appeared Allison's and Randy's lives were

heading in two very different directions until one fateful afternoon when their paths crossed again as Allison was leaving a store on another side of town. She had taken an extra shift in a satellite clinic to help with a staffing shortage. To save time, she ran into a nearby grocery store close to the clinic on her way home. As fate would have it, Randy was walking in as she was walking out. Randy recognized her immediately and called her name. Surprised, Allison greeted him with a warm smile. They chatted briefly and had what she though was a pleasant conversation. Allison left feeling good. She was happy to see Randy doing well. She even told Mark of the encounter later that evening and both were pleased that he was getting on with his life. Little did they know, but that chance encounter reignited Randy's simmering jealousy. Later that evening, Randy drove by their house multiple times, fueled by an inner burning rage that had never really been extinguished. Randy wanted Allison back and was willing to do whatever it took to make that happen.

When Randy pulled into the driveway, he noticed Ryan and one of his bandmates loading something into a car next door. Because Allison was already home, he parked behind her, directly next to where Ryan and James were working. Randy was already agitated and wasn't in the mood to hear Allison complain about him not picking Cindy up from school. If anything, in his mind, Allison owed him an explanation as to why the police showed up at the house to question him about Mark's death. Daniel's visit so enraged him that he spent the day at his buddy Tony's house, trying to smoke and drink that uncomfortable feeling away.

Tony was in some ways a lot like Randy –he was milking an old disability claim from a previous job injury. But unlike Randy, Tony had jumped over all the hurdles and through all the hoops legally to obtain his disability standing. Part of his claim was his need for medical marijuana for his pain. The reality was, Tony didn't do much of anything all day except drink and get high. The perfect buddy for Randy. The two would often spend their days together drinking and smoking while they solved all the world's problems until Randy eventually had to leave.

This day especially, Randy felt the need to hang out with Tony. Daniel's early morning visit had Randy all riled up. By 11a.m., Randy and Tony were right where they wanted to be and stayed that way until late into the afternoon. Randy was so out of it, he completely forgot about Cindy and never heard any of Allison's phone calls. But now, sitting in the driveway at the house, the liquor and pot had long since worn off and that irritated, uncomfortable tension from earlier in the morning was back.

Ryan nodded toward Randy when he got out of his car, but Randy made no effort to return the gesture and started toward the front door. When Randy entered the house, he heard the shower running in their bedroom. He assumed it was Allison since she usually took a shower after getting home from work. Knowing she was going to confront him about forgetting Cindy, he headed to the kitchen to get a beer in an attempt to numb himself for what was sure to come.

Other than the distant sound of the shower running, the house was strangely quiet. Randy briefly wondered where the brat was. Then he heard her. He tilted his head to try to orient himself in the right direction toward where the sound was coming from. Listening intently, he could hear giggling coming from the backyard. When he opened the kitchen door, it was confirmed. He could hear Cindy down by the creek. It sounded like she was having a good time.

Hearing Cindy at play irritated Randy. The longer he stood there listening, the angrier he became. One small pleasure he got from living in the house with the two of them, was tormenting Cindy. Mistreating and harassing Mark's daughter seemed to satisfy some morbid inner desire. Even though Cindy had long since become immune to Randy's harsh remarks, he still got a sick satisfaction out of being cruel to her.

Randy took a long swig from his beer. Spilling some down his chin, he stood in the open doorway looking out. A twisted smile formed on his face. With his free hand he wiped the beer from his chin and then exited the house in Cindy's direction.

Chapter 13

Cindy and the kittens had only known each other for a few days but it was obvious that the three were becoming very close. The kittens showed no fear around Cindy. They had even taken to climbing into her lap and letting her pick them up. Cindy loved holding them and stroking their tiny heads and bodies. She was especially careful not to show any favoritism toward one or the other and tried to spend equal amounts of time holding and playing with both kittens.

The string Cindy brought with her was especially popular with the little ones. She would dragged it around and the kittens liked chasing after it at full speed. She also had several multicolored small rubber balls for them to play with. O was especially fond of a shiny pink one with sparkles. Sitting on the creek bank, Cindy had become good at balancing her attention between the two. At the moment, Buddy wanted to chase the string on one side of her while O preferred his little shiny ball. Cindy blindly tossed the ball behind her while playing tug-of-war with Buddy. Immediately little O shot off after the ball as fast as his tiny legs would carry him. Unknown to Cindy and the kittens, Randy had quietly approached and was standing about 10 feet behind her. The ball came to a stop against his left boot. Completely fixated on the ball, O chased after it, unaware of the danger he was running into…

"What the hell is this?" Randy demanded as he snatched little O right off the ground.

Cindy jumped up and turned around all in the same motion. Buddy was startled by the stranger and ran into some nearby underbrush.

"Don't hurt him!" Cindy pleaded. Her eyes were huge. She knew Randy wouldn't hesitate for a second to kill the kitten, but she pleaded anyway.

"Does your mother know you've been keeping these rats out here?" His grip was tightening around little O and Cindy could see he was struggling to get free.

"Randy! Please! You're hurting him!"

But her pleas only fell on deaf ears. Randy was enjoying the moment. Seeing her fear and desperation, hearing her pleading for the kitten's life only reinforced his resolve to be cruel. He wanted to inflict maximum emotional damage. Another twisted and grotesque smile appeared on his face.

"Do you know what really happened to your precious dog Biscuit?"

Cindy stood frozen with fear, not knowing what Randy was going to do to little O.

"He wasn't killed by a snake. I snapped the mutt's neck and then tossed him into the creek."

A single tear ran down Cindy's cheek. She knew with that, O didn't stand a chance. She knew pleading would be useless at this point. She just hoped whatever Randy did would be quick and O wouldn't suffer.

Cindy's face became rigid. Her fear was gone. If looks could kill, Randy would be dead on the ground. "Monster," she said. Her eyes were locked on him. Showing no fear, she again repeated herself. "You're a monster."

Randy was momentarily taken aback. He wasn't expecting this from Cindy. She wasn't fearful. She wasn't crying or pleading for him to release the kitten. This wasn't the reaction he wanted. Angered, Randy extended the arm with O in it back as far as he could and then threw him as hard as he could like a baseball across the backyard toward the rock garden.

Cindy watched as O disappeared into the distance. She then locked eyes on Randy. For a second, the intensity of her gaze caught him by surprise, her eyes reflecting the rage building within her. Facing Randy, Cindy screamed the most bloodcurdling scream anyone had ever heard, amplified by a year's worth of anger, frustration, and heartache all escaping at once.

Ryan and James were still outside packing some of the band's equipment they would need for their performance the next night into James's car. Hearing Cindy's scream, Ryan froze. The silence was deafening. Immediately the worst came to mind.

"Cindy!" he shouted. In a flash Ryan was around the hedge and racing up Allison's driveway toward the back yard with James doing all he could to keep up.

Allison finished her shower and dressed. As she was walking through the living room, she looked out the large picture window facing the front yard and noticed Randy's car in the driveway. A heavy feeling of dread came over her for a second, but it quickly passed. She knew what she needed to do, and she was determined not to waste any more time. Taking a deep breath, she headed toward the back door to find Cindy so she could get her ready to go Ryan's. While passing through the kitchen she heard Cindy's scream. "Cindy!" Allison cried out as she threw open the back door and raced out of the house.

Randy looked down at Cindy and again smiled his grotesque smile. "Where's the other one?" he demanded as he walked toward the underbrush Buddy ran into. Kicking the bushes hard like a wild man, Randy flushed Buddy out. Cindy screamed again and ran full force into Randy, trying to push him away but only causing him to stagger back toward the creek. Randy still managed to get in one more forceful kick that sent little Buddy tumbling head over tail down the path, badly cutting and breaking his right front leg in the process. Little Buddy tried to escape, but his broken leg wouldn't cooperate.

In her attempt to shove Randy, Cindy bounced off him and fell to the ground behind the bench. Seeing Buddy injured on the path, she quickly stood up and jumped between him and a rapidly approaching Randy. In that moment, she didn't care what happened to her. She just knew she was going to do everything possible to protect the helpless kitten from the rapidly approaching maniac. Bracing for impact, Cindy stood her ground, fearless.

Out of nowhere Tor landed on the concrete bench, startling Randy and halting his approach. Tor's eyes were ablaze with a blinding yellow-green glow. Tail twitching, teeth bared, he hissed and then let out a ferocious growl that would have stopped a lion in its tracks. From Cindy's view point, Tor looked like a panther ready to destroy its prey.

"What the F…" Randy started, but Tor swung at him with such speed he never saw it coming. The impact threw Randy back about 10 feet onto the creek bank. He felt like he'd been hit with a sledgehammer and was momentarily weakened and dazed.

Cindy briefly froze. She couldn't believe what she just saw. With Randy temporarily incapacitated, Tor jumped off the bench and scooped Buddy up in his mouth. Cindy followed and they raced up the path as fast as they could go.

The path wound its way from the creek along the edge of the property and through the dense foliage close to Ryan's property line. When Tor rounded a sharp turn in the path, he darted off through the underbrush in the direction Randy had thrown O. Cindy rounded the curve just seconds later, but Tor was gone. For a brief second, she paused, wondering where he went, but then she heard Randy. He'd recovered and was rapidly approaching.

Hearing her mom's panicked call, Cindy shouted back, "Mommy!" Then she took off in her direction as fast as she could go.

Allison ran to the edge of the pool deck just as Cindy emerged from the wooded path. Cindy ran into her mom's arms. "He's coming! He's coming!" she screamed, while trying to pull her mom toward the house in a panic.

"Who Baby? Who's coming?" Allison asked, trying to calm her. Just then, Randy emerged from the path. He was out of breath and clearly angry. Cindy noticed the scratches on his arm.

"What did you do to my daughter?" Allison demanded.

Before he could answer, Ryan and James burst through the side gate, joining them on the pool deck. Ryan stood beside Allison and James behind Ryan. Both men had ice-cold expressions. All Allison had to do was give the word and they'd take care of Randy with pleasure.

Randy ignored Ryan and James, addressing Allison.

"Your daughter has been keeping stray cats down by the creek! That explains why everything out here smells like cat piss. I took care of the problem," he said with his typical arrogance.

"He killed one of them! He threw him across the yard and then he tried to stomp the other one! He told me he's the one who killed Biscuit. He said it wasn't a snake bite; it was him! He broke Biscuit's neck and threw him into the creek! You're a monster!" Cindy shouted, stepping out from behind her mom. She wasn't the least bit afraid. Ryan stepped up and stood next to Cindy. James did the same. It was obvious both men wanted to beat the hell out of Randy.

Fortunately for Randy, Allison spoke out.

"Get your things and get out of my house!" she ordered.

"But Allison—" he started to say.

She cut him off. "I don't want to hear it. We're over, Randy. Get your things and get out!" she demanded.

Ryan and James stepped up again in a protective gesture.

Normally Randy would have protested or even begged and pleaded for her to give him another chance, but with Ryan and James standing there, his ego got the better of him. Outnumbered, he knew it was in his best interest to go, for now. Filled with an inner burning rage, Randy pushed past them and went into the house to gather his things.

Allison kneeled down and hugged Cindy tightly. "I'm so sorry baby! I'm so sorry," she kept repeating as she lovingly held Cindy in her arms, thankful she was not hurt.

Cindy held her back. Overcome with emotion, Cindy burst into tears. "We have to find Buddy Mommy, he's out there somewhere and he's hurt bad," Cindy said, pleading for them to go look.

"Ok babe, we'll go look for him right after we deal with Randy," Allison said, holding her tight and gently rocking her.

സ≈

Randy didn't have much to claim as his own. When he moved in, he didn't bring anything with him except clothes and a cardboard box about the size of a shoe box filled with a few personal items. He quickly packed his clothes into a large duffel bag and then went to the closet to retrieve the box. When he moved in, he put the box on the top shelf of their bedroom closet for safe keeping. He quickly opened the lid to check the contents. Reaching in, he pulled out a .38 caliber handgun and smiled before mumbling out loud, "This isn't over yet, bitch." Hearing them entering the house, Randy quickly put the gun back in the box and closed the lid. He packed the box in the duffel bag with his other belongings.

Allison and Cindy waited in the kitchen while Ryan and James stood in the living room. Randy didn't say a word as he blew by them on his way to the car.

After Randy stormed out, Ryan and James stayed with Allison and Cindy for a while longer. Cindy insisted they go back out and search for Buddy because it was starting to get dark and she knew he was injured. They searched the path and fort but found nothing. Finally, they were forced to call off the search when it became too dark. Ryan called a twenty-four-hour locksmith to come change the locks and he ordered dinner for everyone while they waited.

Chapter 14

When Tor rounded the sharp bend on the path, he shot off into the overgrown yard. He sensed it was safe to leave Cindy after hearing her mom call to her from the pool deck. He could also feel Ryan's approach. He couldn't physically see Ryan, but he knew he was close. Thanks to a prior encounter with Ryan some months ago, they were linked in a way only Tor could understand. It was this connection that drew Tor to Ryan originally. But hearing Cindy crying on the bench that fateful day and then rescuing her from the water moccasin, Tor temporarily altered his plans. Feeling Ryan's approaching presence, he knew Cindy would be safe. O and Buddy were his priorities now. Tor could sense O was fading quickly and knew he needed to find him before it was too late.

Guided by an inner sense, Tor closed in on O's fading life force. He could hear his tiny heart slowing and could feel his energy fading as he raced across the yard. Leaping out of the brush, Tor landed in an open area of the rock garden still carrying Buddy in his mouth. He quickly dropped Buddy on the ground and approached O's crumpled lifeless body lying in the weeds and gravel. He was barely breathing. Through partially opened eyes, little O let out a faint whimper when Tor approached. He was badly broken. Between Randy squeezing the life from him and the force of the impact, it was a miracle he was still alive.

Tor softly sniffed his twisted, battered body. Feeling Tor's presence, O managed one last faint whimper before falling unconscious.

Buddy sat close, his eyes huge. He knew his brother was in trouble. He himself was bleeding and broken, but for the moment, he sat quietly out of the way, observing.

Tor's eyes ignited in a brilliant yellow-green glow. He moved close to O and exhaled a smoky stream of yellow-green energy. Gradually, the stream became more solid. With every ragged breath O took, more of the smoky energy was absorbed. The more energy he took in, the better his breathing became. As Tor's energy freely flowed through O's broken body, it concentrated on the damaged areas. His broken ribs and ruptured organs began repairing themselves as the energy flowed. After a few minutes, Tor shut his eyes to extinguish the glow. When he opened them, they were normal.

Within seconds of Tor cutting off the flow, little O started to regain consciousness. His eyes fluttered open and he excitedly cried out before leaping to his feet. Buddy hobbled over to his brother and to the best of his ability, rubbed affectionately against him. Tor knew Buddy was also injured and again ignited his eyes. Buddy stood still, almost as if he knew what to do. Tor approached. When they were practically nose to nose, he exhaled the same energy stream. As Buddy absorbed the life force, his cut started glowing that same brilliant yellow-green color. It tingled, but Buddy remained still and let Tor's healing energy do its work. Within seconds, his broken leg was repaired, and the glowing cut had healed itself. Again, Tor shut his eyes and extinguished the flow.

Tor opened his eyes just in time to see an excited Buddy and O racing toward him before embracing him with enthusiastic affection. He stood in place, letting the grateful brothers climb on him for a few more seconds before walking a short distance and lying down on the edge of the clearing where he watched the boys play. The sun was going down and soon it would be dark. Tor let the boys play a little while longer before leading them back to the cave for the evening.

Tor was exhausted. He'd expended a large amount of energy knocking Randy back and healing the boys. He needed to get them safely situated in the cave so he could go out later and replenish his energy. From inside the cave, Tor could hear Cindy and the others over by the fort looking for Buddy. Tor knew what needed to be done, but that would have to wait until the morning. For now, they were safe.

After dinner, Ryan excused himself and James. They still had things to do in order to prepare for tomorrow night's show. Allison and Cindy again thanked the guys for all their help. Cindy hugged Ryan especially tight.

"Thank you for being here tonight," Cindy said, tearing up. "Tomorrow morning, if you have time, will you help me find O? I want to give him a proper burial," she said, sniffling, while trying to be strong.

Ryan hugged her back and nodded, trying to fight an overwhelming sense of emotion himself. "Of course I will. And we'll look around again for the other one, too. If he's out there, we'll find him," he said, trying to reassure her.

Earlier in the evening, after Randy left, Cindy had them

all out in the backyard looking for Buddy until it got too dark. She was heartbroken to give up the search and made them promise to look again in the morning.

Cindy nodded her head in agreement, trying to be positive, but she had her doubts. Randy had kicked Buddy hard. She saw Tor pick him up, but she wasn't sure if he was still alive or not. After another round of goodbyes, Allison told Cindy to get ready for bed while she walked Ryan and James out.

Standing on the front porch, Allison shut the door so Cindy could not overhear what she had to say.

"Guys, I can't thank you enough for all your help tonight. I'm just so glad you were here. I never thought he'd go this far. Killing kittens? Telling Cindy he broke Biscuit's neck, then threw him into the creek! What kind of sick monster does that?" Her lip was quivering as she tried to fight back emotions. "How was I so oblivious to it all? Why didn't I see it? And then watching Cindy almost drown in the creek—"

Ryan cut her off and pulled her to him with an embracing hug.

"Enough. What's done is done. The priority now is seeing to you and that little girl in there. You've both been through a lot and getting rid of that asshole is an excellent first step in the right direction."

Allison smiled and wiped a tear from her eye. She nodded her head in agreement as she regained composure. They again said goodnight and Allison went back inside the house.

"Do you really think that's the last they'll see of that prick?" James asked.

Ryan shook his head and sighed. "I doubt it. He went too easy. I have a feeling he'll be back."

"I'm glad I don't have this kind of drama with my neighbors," James joked.

ৎৣৎৣ

After the kittens fell asleep, Tor slipped out of the cave. He was driven by an urge only he could understand. For the next several hours he hunted along the creek and between the other nearby properties. He was careful not to go too far away. Rats, mice, snakes, and frogs were all on the menu. He was driven by both a nutritional hunger and a need to replenish his energy reserves. In a few hours, he returned to the cave, revitalized. Careful not to disturb the little ones, Tor curled around them in a protective embrace. O briefly opened his eyes and made a low-pitched squeak while stretching, then nuzzled against Tor. Content, little O drifted off to sleep with a smile on his face.

ৎৣৎৣ

Allison kissed Cindy good night before tucking her into bed. It had been a long day for the both of them. Besides all the drama with Randy, Allison had worked long hours throughout the week, and it was now catching up with her. She had been ready to call it a night for some time, but didn't want to leave Cindy alone, so she laid down on the bed next to her. They talked for a little while about the kittens and the possibility of getting new ones in the future until Allison's exhaustion caught up with her.

As Allison slept, Cindy laid there holding her favorite stuffed animal and staring at the shapes her nightlight was casting on the ceiling. She was restless, but didn't want to disturb her mom. This was the first time in a long time that Allison stayed in her room. Still, Cindy couldn't help but think of Mr. Kitty and how he sprung to the rescue. And those eyes. They were glowing so bright. How was that even possible, she wondered? She'd never seen anything like it. He looked so ferocious. Then, when she remembered how Randy was knocked back by his scratch, she smiled. Still, she wondered how he did that. Why were his eyes glowing so bright? The event played over and over in her head as the night slowly rolled on. For whatever reason, she didn't mention anything about Mr. Kitty to her mom or the guys. She knew it was real, but wasn't sure how to explain it, so she kept that part to herself. Finally, the events of the day caught up with her, and she too drifted off to sleep, curled up next to her mom.

Chapter 15

At dawn, Tor had the kittens up. His internal clock knew Cindy would be awake soon. Instead of leading them to the creek bank where they usually waited for Cindy, he led them to the back door off the kitchen. The kittens were particularly rambunctious this morning. Having both received large infusions of energy, their bodies craved the nutrients necessary to turn that energy into nutritious fuel they could use. Plainly put, they were hungry.

Full of themselves, the kittens playfully swatted and chased acorns around the pool deck as Tor looked on. Finally, Tor knew it was time. He approached the boys and his eyes began to glow softly. The kittens immediately became calm and sat facing him. Through an exchange of energy, an understanding was reached. When Tor's eyes returned to normal, the boys ran over and rubbed affectionately against him, both expressing their gratitude and sorrow. For they knew he was leaving. Hearing movement inside the house, Tor again flashed his eyes at the boys before disappearing into the underbrush. The boys settled down and waited by the steps leading to the kitchen as directed. Little did they know, their lives were about to change forever.

Hearing birds singing as they were waking up to meet

the new day, Cindy's eyes fluttered open. It was early Saturday morning and the sun was just beginning to rise. Cindy quietly climbed out of bed, being especially careful not to wake her mom. After quickly dressing, she made her way to the back door. She knew Tor was still out there and wanted to find him and thank him if he was still around. She was worried Randy might have frightened him off. When Cindy opened the door, she screamed again. But this time, with delight.

"Buddy! O!" she shouted. Cindy shot down the steps and carefully picked them up. Hugging them affectionately, she couldn't believe it. She was sure O had been killed and didn't know what had happened to Buddy. She was so relieved, she kissed the boys over and over while crying tears of joy.

Hearing all the commotion, Allison suddenly appeared at the back door. Disheveled and still not fully awake, it took her a few seconds to take in the scene. When she saw Cindy with the kittens, her heart melted. Seeing her daughter so happy made her burst into tears of joy.

Appearing out of nowhere, Ryan came running through the side gate. He'd just returned home from his morning run when he heard Cindy cry out. When he noticed the kittens, a smile a mile-wide appeared on his face. He walked over and joined them on the deck.

"I bet they're hungry, do you have any of that food left?" Ryan asked, squatting down next to Cindy and gently rubbing the boys' little heads.

Cindy's eyes lit up and she nodded her head enthusiastically. She shoved one kitten into Ryan's hands and the other into her mom's. "I'll be right back," she said, then shot off down the path to retrieve the food from the storage box at the end of the trail.

Allison looked at Ryan and asked, "How did you know she had food?" The smirk on her face made him smile.

Humbled, he lowered his head, pretending to be guilty, "I choose not to answer on the grounds that I might incriminate myself."

Allison squinted her eyes and shook her head before breaking out with a huge smile. "They are cute little guys, aren't they?" she said, rubbing O's tiny head with her finger.

Cindy was back in a flash with the bag of food.

"Well, let's bring these little guys inside. They might as well get used to their new home," Allison said, as she led the group up the steps and into the kitchen.

After an evening of heavy drinking and smoking, Randy crashed at Tony's place for the night. Over the years, this had become the routine. When women Randy lived with finally wised up and kicked him out, Tony's was the first place he'd go.

When Randy woke up that morning, he immediately knew something was wrong. His left arm was throbbing with pain. The scratch marks Tor made had turned black and looked infected. He tried washing out the wounds, but the pain was excruciating. Finally, he decided to drive himself to the emergency room.

"A cat did this?" the doctor asked, not believing it.

"Yes, a cat did it. It scratched me yesterday. When I woke up this morning, it looked like this," Randy barked.

The doctor was confused. Smelling the strong odor of pot and alcohol, he figured Randy probably had trouble with memory. The wounds looked weeks old to him and far worse than a cat scratch. The tissue around the lacerations was dead. It had decomposed and was borderline gangrenous. Concerned about infection, the doctor conferred with other emergency room professionals. They all agreed he would need immediate surgery to remove the dead and dying tissue before it became even more toxic, at which point he could lose his arm and maybe even his life.

Randy became irate. He wasn't going to let them do surgery on him for a cat scratch! He knew the incident just happened the previous evening. For the doctor to think it was weeks old was crazy. He figured the doctor was just attempting to make a quick buck by trying to convince him to have a surgical procedure he didn't really need. Irritated, Randy left the ER against the advice of the medical staff.

Sitting in his car in the parking lot, Randy noticed the cardboard box on the floorboard in front of the passenger seat. He reached down and placed the box on the seat. Flipping open the lid, he took the gun out and held it in his hand. Speaking out loud he said, "You and me have some unfinished business, cat. First, I take care of the brat and her mother and then I'm going to take care of you." Instead of putting the gun back in the box, Randy slid it under his seat, started the car, and headed toward Allison's.

Chapter 16

Since the previous day's encounter with Randy went so well, Detective Baxter decided to pay him another visit. Daniel was also looking forward to seeing Allison again and hoped she would be home this time. He really wasn't that surprised she didn't call him. Even though it had only been a day, for some reason he figured Randy never passed on his message.

Given that it was Saturday, Daniel didn't drop by as early as the previous day. This time he wanted to be more considerate for Allison's sake. Still, he was looking forward to questioning Randy in her presence. He was curious if he'd get the same arrogance with Allison there.

As Daniel approached the house, he did not see Randy's car. Figuring he'd probably stepped out for something, he decided to park in the driveway anyway. He knew this would irritate Randy when he returned. Smiling, he pulled in and parked. Daniel got out of his car and again started whistling the same happy-go-lucky tune as he put on a coat and walked up the sidewalk toward the front door.

Just as he reached the top step of the porch, the door opened. A well-built, shirtless athletic man stepped out wearing only running shorts and shoes. Startled, the detective froze. *Was Allison seeing someone behind Randy's back?*

Ryan immediately recognized Daniel from his gym.

"Detective Baxter, this is a surprise," Ryan said, greeting him warmly. They went to the same health club and sometimes worked out together. Allison was right behind Ryan.

"Daniel! This is an unexpected surprise," she said with a huge smile. Allison then realized how awkward this might look seeing a shirtless Ryan leaving her house and quickly introduced him as her next-door neighbor.

"We know each other from our gym. Good to see you, Daniel. What brings you to our quiet little neighborhood this morning?" Ryan asked, innocently enough.

Hesitating for a moment, Daniel answered, "I didn't mean to interrupt you guys, but I was hoping to follow up on a few things from our conversation the other day. But if this isn't a good time, I can come back," he said, a little disappointed, but also trying to respect Allison's privacy in regard to what he thought might be going on between her and Ryan.

"That won't be necessary. This character was just leaving," Allison said, smiling warmly to Daniel and playfully pushing Ryan toward the steps.

Ryan could tell there was an attraction between them. "Yes, I still have a million things to do before the show tonight. If you guys are looking for something to do later, you're welcome to come this evening. It's going to be our largest performance to date, and it should be a pretty good one too. We're introducing several new songs. I think you guys would like them," Ryan said.

"You're in a band too? I knew you were some hot-shot advertising guy, but I didn't know you were in a band," Daniel said, surprised.

"Oh yes. Ryan has the most amazing voice. They're really good. Mark and I used to go to their shows all the time."

"I'm impressed. A jack of all trades," Daniel added, still unsure how to read the situation.

"Well, if you guys want to come, just let me know. I'll leave word at the door to let you in as my guests. Now if you'll excuse me, I still have work to do for my real job before I can go play rock star. Good to see you, Daniel." Ryan looked at Allison and said, "And tell your daughter enough with all the screaming." He winked and smiled at Allison.

She smiled back and said, "Thanks again Ryan. We're really grateful for all your help."

"Anytime," Ryan said, waving as he walked back toward his house. He could tell Allison was excited to see Daniel. Smiling to himself, he said out loud, "I think Randy might have some competition."

৯৽৵৶

Unknown to all of them, Randy was parked down the street behind a neighbor's truck. From his vantage point, he could see the three of them talking on the front porch. Seeing Ryan and Daniel infuriated him. Allison was his and he'd be damned if some muscle stud or another damn cop was going to take her away from him. Holding the gun, he thought about just walking right up to them, but then thought better of it. Ryan didn't like him, and Officer Baxter was most likely armed. No, he'd wait for another time. His arm was also aching, so he decided to go back to Tony's and self-medicate before planning the next move. Starting the car, Randy backed up and turned around in a neighbor's driveway, careful not to be seen by Allison or the detective.

ల౷౽

Allison walked Daniel to the kitchen where Cindy was playing with the kittens and made the introductions.

"What have we here?" Daniel asked, squatting down but being careful to keep a respectful distance. He didn't want to frighten the boys.

Cindy scooped up Buddy and O and enthusiastically made her own introductions. "This is O, and this is Buddy," she said, holding them up. Both were being unusually calm this morning. Normally they were a lot jumpier, even with her. Clearly something had changed, but she didn't think too much about it. She figured they were probably more relaxed now that they knew they had a safe place to live and someone to take care of them.

"Wow! What handsome fellows," Daniel said, gently reaching out to pet them. "They look so little. How long have you had them?" he asked, still softly patting their heads.

"They showed up a few days ago. I've been taking care of them ever since," Cindy answered proudly.

Allison cleared her throat. "So young lady, I have to ask. How did Ryan know about that bag of food you had in your fort?"

Cindy just smiled as she carefully put the kittens back down on the kitchen floor. She looked up at her mom and shrugged, still smiling. "I don't know," she finally said.

Allison chuckled and patted her on the head. "Ok young lady, can you excuse us? I'm going to take Officer Baxter to the den so we can talk."

Cindy's eyes got big. "You're a police officer? Did you know my daddy?" she asked. Allison had not introduced Daniel as a policeman, just by his name.

"Why yes, I did. Your dad and I met when we were going through the police academy together." Daniel didn't take it any further. He wanted to keep the conversation with Cindy as positive as possible.

Cindy again smiled, but this time she beamed with pride. "It's nice to meet you Officer Baxter," she said, standing at attention and extending her hand for him to shake. Daniel didn't hesitate. He shook her hand and said, "Likewise young lady. It's very nice to meet you, too."

Allison told Cindy she'd go to the store for cat litter and anything else they'd need for the kittens just as soon as she was finished talking with Daniel. But in the meantime, she asked if she would keep the kittens in the kitchen in case of any accidents. Cindy was excited that her mom was being so accepting of Buddy and O. She was not only relieved she was going to be able to keep them, but she was also happy to see her mom excited about the kittens. Still, she couldn't help but think about Mr. Kitty. Why wasn't he out there with the kittens this morning too, she wondered?

Once her mom and Daniel went to the den, Cindy quickly gathered up the boys and put them in the large box her mom had found. She set them up with food and water, then quietly scooped out some dry kitten food to take with her before sneaking out the back door in search of Mr. Kitty.

৽৽৶

Allison showed Daniel to a chair in the den, and they both sat down and got more comfortable. "I must say I was surprised to find you on our front porch this morning," Allison said, starting the conversation.

"I hope I wasn't interrupting anything between you and Ryan," Daniel said, attempting to feel out the situation.

Allison burst into laughter. "Ryan?" She questioned, still laughing and shaking her head, while rolling her eyes.

"Well...I just assumed..." He paused, trying to understand why she found the assumption so funny.

"I hope you're better at being a detective than that," she joked.

Daniel remained quiet and just looked at her.

"You saw him leaving here this morning without a shirt and thought we had something going on?" she asked, still amused. "That's just Ryan. He spends more time shirtless than any man I know. There's not a married or unmarried woman in this neighborhood who doesn't like to watch the 'Ryan Show' when he goes out for his morning run. And that's to say nothing of the never-ending parade of women going in and out of his house in the evenings," she joked behind a sly smile.

Daniel shook his head. It was obvious by her tone that there wasn't anything going on between them, but he was humored by Allison's commentary.

"But seriously, Mark and I became good friends with Ryan and his band. We all used to be pretty close until Randy..." Her words trailed off. She shook her head and added, "Ryan was another casualty of my impulsive decision to let Randy move in so soon after Mark's passing."

Allison paused, gathering her thoughts before continuing. "Randy didn't like Ryan. I think he was intimidated by him. For one, as you can see, he's in great shape and never wears a shirt," she smiled before continuing. "But mostly I think he was jealous. He would always get so mad when he saw me or Cindy talking to Ryan. I hated that. Cindy and Ryan had been close ever since she was born and he was so sweet to her after Mark passed. But once Randy moved in, everything changed. It just became easier to keep our distance from Ryan in order to keep the peace in the home."

Allison slightly shook her head as she looked out the large sliding glass doors in the den. Daniel could tell she was in deep thought and remained quiet. He wanted to let her choose the necessary words in her own time.

"I'm just so fortunate Ryan didn't turn his back on us like we did on him. Especially these past several days. He literally saved Cindy's life once this week and then last night he and his friend James came to our rescue yet again," she added, exhaling a notable sigh of relief. "As badly as I treated him, he was still there for us. Ryan is indeed a good friend. One I'm very fortunate to have as my neighbor."

Daniel was intrigued. Curious, he now had an opportunity to inquire about Randy.

"Speaking of Randy, did he happen to mention that I dropped by yesterday?"

"You did? No, he didn't. But to be fair, he didn't have much time to say anything before I asked him to leave."

"You asked him to leave? Might I ask why?"

Allison looked at him straight on.

"Because it was time."

∽∾

Cindy walked down the winding path calling for her friend, but saw no sign of him. She was concerned but couldn't shake an overwhelming feeling that she was being watched. She felt like he was out there somewhere, so she called several more times, but still nothing. Standing by the bench, she shut her eyes and then spoke out loud.

"I don't know if you can hear me or even if I'll ever see you again Mr. Kitty, but I wanted to thank you for saving my life and the kittens. I don't know how you did it, but I know somehow you fixed Buddy and O. I saw what Randy did to them and now they're all better. I also saw how you scratched Randy and knocked him down. You saved all of our lives, and I just wanted to thank you for that. I promise to give your little friends a good home. And please know, if you ever need a place to stay, you're always welcome to stay with us."

When Cindy finished speaking, she opened her eyes. As she stood on the creek bank a gentle breeze blew through her hair. She smiled. Somehow Cindy knew Mr. Kitty had heard and appreciated everything she said. She also understood that he had to be going. He was on a mission, and it was time for him to be on his way. "Thank you, Mr. Kitty, I will never forget you," she said out loud.

Cindy left the food on the ground next to the bench and then ran back up the path to the house. When she reached the top step, she paused and turned toward the backyard. Looking out across the pool Cindy focused on the dense underbrush running along the creek and smiled again before going inside to be with the boys.

Tor did hear her. He heard every word she said. Laying concealed in the brush, he watched and listened as Cindy spoke. Randy was gone and Buddy and O were now safe and had a home. It was time for him to continue on the original mission. After Cindy ran back inside the house, Tor consumed the food she'd left by the bench. When he was finished, he followed the path along the fence until he found the opening between the yards. Hesitating for a second, he listened. He could hear Cindy's high-pitched laugh as she played with the boys in the kitchen. Satisfied all was well, he sniffed the clean morning air before passing through the opening into Ryan's backyard.

Chapter 17

Allison and Daniel sat talking in the den for a good part of the morning. Fortunately, it was Saturday. Allison had arranged to have as many weekends off as possible for the foreseeable future. She was determined to be there for Cindy, especially in light of recent events. It was time for her to start being a mom again.

As a detective, Daniel's schedule was more flexible. Since his wife passed, he found working helped fill some of the void her loss left. He also knew he'd rattled Randy the previous day and wanted to follow up when Allison would be home. Coming back the next morning was technically "off the clock," but he felt the visit would be worth his time. And in all honesty, he was looking forward to seeing Allison again.

Allison caught Daniel up on the week's events. Daniel was particularly interested in Cindy's creek incident and listened intently as Allison recalled what happened.

"At first I couldn't believe Randy would want to hurt Cindy," Allison said, shaking her head in disbelief. "But after standing in the same spot where I saw Randy standing and then talking with Ryan, I'm convinced now." By her expression, Daniel could tell there was no doubt in her mind.

"You can see where Cindy was struggling in the creek perfectly from where he was hiding in the brush. And Ryan said when he came around the bend on his boat, he could also see Randy standing on the creek bank just watching. Ryan later asked Cindy what she was doing on the dock, and she told him she went out there to retrieve her coloring box. Somehow it had found its way to the end of the dock!" Allison briefly paused. Daniel could tell she was getting angry retelling the event. "I'm sure Randy put it there. Ryan's guests fished the box out of the creek. Too bad we can't check it for fingerprints or something to prove it." Allison sat quiet for a moment. Recalling the event brought back the emotion of the day. And knowing what she now knew, it also brought out her anger.

"What kind of sick monster just stands there watching a little girl drowning in front of him?" Allison asked. Her eyes were burning with the rage of a protective mother.

Daniel diligently took notes as Allison recalled the event. His mind was racing. After questioning Randy the previous day, he was convinced Randy had something to do with Mark's death, but he also knew he would need a lot more evidence than just "a feeling." As he listened to Allison, he contemplated telling her of his own suspicions regarding Randy's possible involvement in Mark's murder. He wondered if she might know more than she realized.

"And then last night..." Allison paused to collect her thoughts. The den was dead quiet. Hearing Cindy playing with the kittens in the kitchen, she continued.

"I got a call yesterday from Cindy's school informing me that she had not been picked up. Randy usually does this, but sometimes he forgets. I called him but got no answer. I tried a few more times and still nothing. So, I picked her up and came home. When we arrived at the house, Randy was still not home. Ryan pulled in his driveway a few seconds after we did." Allison paused, thinking for a second before adding, "I'm so thankful he arrived when he did."

Daniel could tell she was doing her best to recall everything as accurately as possible. She continued. "After Cindy ran inside, I spoke with Ryan. I wanted to see if Cindy could stay with him that evening while I confronted Randy. I told Ryan I was going to ask Randy to leave and didn't want Cindy to go through that. Having dealt with him in the past, I knew there was a good chance I might have to call the police. Ryan said it was ok and to send her over any time. We then discussed the creek incident and what he saw from his boat before jumping in and saving Cindy." Allison teared up.

Daniel reached over and squeezed her hand. "It's ok Allison, take your time," he said, still holding her hand gently.

"I'm just so thankful Ryan arrived when he did. If he hadn't rescued her, I'm sure she would have drowned out there," Allison said, pointing out the window toward the creek.

Daniel could see by her expression that she had no doubts about the outcome.

Allison squeezed Daniel's hand back and smiled, then continued. "After talking with Ryan, I came inside to shower and change. Cindy went to her fort to feed the kittens she'd been keeping without my knowledge." Allison couldn't help but smile. "After I changed and was walking through the living room I noticed Randy's car in the driveway. I won't deny I wasn't looking forward to the confrontation, but knew it must be done. As I was walking to the back door to get Cindy, I heard her scream the loudest most blood-curdling scream. My heart sank. Immediately I thought the worst and ran to her."

Daniel was on the edge of his seat. All his years of being a detective still doesn't fully prepare one for the job. And having a personal connection to this case just made it that much harder. "What happened next?" Daniel asked, completely out of character. Gone was his calm detective persona. He was speaking in the tone of a concerned friend.

This was not missed by Allison, and she continued. "Cindy ran up the path and right into my arms. She was terrified and was desperately trying to get me to go inside. Around the same time Ryan and James busted through the side fence. They'd heard Cindy's scream from the front yard. When Randy emerged from the path, I could tell he was very angry. Cindy immediately accused him of killing her kittens and told us Randy boasted to her that he broke our dog Biscuit's neck and threw him into the creek last year." Again, Allison paused collecting herself. "Cindy was fearless and so brave. I didn't doubt her for a second," Allison added, sitting up in her chair. It was obvious to Daniel how proud she was of Cindy's courage.

"How did Randy handle Cindy's accusations?" Daniel asked. Hearing of the murdered dog only further solidified his suspicions.

"He didn't deny anything. He told me Cindy had been keeping stray cats behind my back and that he took care of it. His tone was so cold it made my skin crawl. When I heard that, I must have channeled some of Cindy's strength into myself because the next thing I remember saying to Randy was to get out. I told him we were through. He tried to say something, but I cut him off. Ryan and James stepped up, which I think intimidated him. They stayed with us while Randy gathered his things and then left."

Allison was quiet for a second before adding, "Knowing what I know now, I'm so glad the guys were here. If they hadn't shown up when they did, I have a bad feeling things would have turned out very different for Cindy and me."

After listening to everything Allison was telling him, Daniel decided to share his suspicions about Randy and Mark. Maybe she could recall something they might have missed earlier in the investigation.

Tor was enjoying a lazy morning stretched out on a comfortable seat cushion in Ryan's boat. The boat was raised out of the water and protected under a roof, but the rest of the boathouse was open. The entire dock and boathouse was sheltered under the canopy of a large oak tree leaning out over the creek. From Ryan's house, only the top of the boathouse could be seen. Well hidden, Tor stood and stretched before changing positions and laying back down on the cushion. From inside the boat, he could hear a lot of activity at Ryan's that morning. Ryan's bandmates had arrived and were loading the last of their equipment into a box truck they'd rented for the show that evening. Ryan had a three-car garage, and one bay was used to store some of the equipment they needed for performances. The activity didn't bother Tor. In fact, he was quite accustomed to the noise, but for now, he chose to keep a distance. Some inner instinct left Tor with an unsettled feeling. For now, he was content observing from afar. When the time was right, he'd make his presence known to Ryan.

Daniel informed Allison that Randy had worked at the abandoned house where Mark was shot. That was not necessarily a smoking gun, but it was a connection. He also told her he'd done a background check on Randy and saw where other women had problems with him before and after they were together. But he confessed that the biggest mystery was motive. Why did he wait six years to do anything? What was the trigger that suddenly set him off after such a long period of time?

Allison sat quietly contemplating all Daniel had told her. The thought that she'd been living with her husband's killer all these months was frightening. Allison's mind was racing. Then suddenly she looked at Daniel. Her eyes were huge. "Oh my god, I think I know what it was!"

When Randy returned to Tony's he was irate. Seeing Ryan leaving the house and the detective arrive sent him into a rage. "She's a whore!" he shouted at Tony. "Nothing but a damn whore!" Selectively editing major parts of the story, Randy told Tony an extravagant tale of deception whereby he painted himself as an innocent victim. He accused Allison of never being faithful to him. The drunker and more stoned he got, the more of an unfaithful deceptive slut Allison became. For hours they drank and smoked. Usually this calmed Randy. But as the day passed, his inner burning jealousy only grew hotter.

Allison's silence was deafening as she sat motionless, replaying an incident over in her mind. Daniel was bursting to know what it was, but remained patient. If she remembered something important, he wanted her to be sure. Allison looked at Daniel.

"I do remember something. A few days before Mark was killed, I ran into Randy as I was leaving a store across town. I'd taken some extra shifts at a clinic over there and on my way home I stopped off at a nearby grocery store. On my way out of the store, I heard someone call my name and when I looked up, it was Randy. We talked briefly and he said he was doing well, and seemed genuinely happy for me. I thought the conversation was very pleasant. I even told Mark about it later that evening and we were both happy that he was doing well." She shook her head. 'I'd completely forgotten about that," her voice trailed off.

Daniel thought for a moment. He didn't want to say anything to alarm Allison any more than she already was, but he couldn't help but think somehow that encounter must have been a catalyst for events to come.

"Does Randy own a gun?"

"Yes. He showed it to me when he first moved in. He

wanted me to know where it was in case I ever needed it. We agreed to keep it in a box on the top shelf of the bedroom closet so Cindy couldn't find it."

Literally a smoking gun, Daniel thought to himself. "Do you know if it's still there?" he asked, hopeful of the response.

Allison quickly stood up. "I don't know, let's see," she said, leading him to the bedroom closet.

"Damn! It's gone." Allison said, looking at the spot where the box had been kept all these months. "He must have taken it with him when he left!" Clearly frustrated, she kicked the closet door.

"Do you know where he might have gone?" Daniel asked, still hopeful.

"Yes, to his friend Tony's. He's gone there before when we've had problems. I don't have the address, but I can tell you where it is."

Daniel scribbled down the directions Allison gave him. Eager to confirm Randy's whereabouts, he stood up. Allison clearly registered a mix of emotions. On the one hand, she was hopeful they might finally have a lead in Mark's case. Yet, on the other, she was horrified to think her husband's killer had been living under their roof the whole time.

Daniel could tell by Allison's expression that she was having a hard time processing everything. He put his hands on her shoulders and pulled her to him. "It's all going to be okay." He hugged her tight. Allison melted into him. For the first time in a year, she truly felt like things were going to be okay. Closing her eyes, she hugged him back. "Thank you,

Daniel. Thank you for caring so much. Something put us in each other's paths for a reason, maybe it was Mark and Connie, I don't know, but something brought us together," she said, still holding him tight.

Daniel was fighting a surge of emotions. Choked up, he managed to say "You and Cindy are going to be okay now. Everything is going to be okay now." As they slowly separated, both hesitated. He wanted to kiss her, but knew this was not the right time. He needed to focus on matters at hand first. Before he left, he told Allison if Randy showed up, not to let him into the house under any circumstances, to call him and the police immediately, then handed her his card. Allison understood and agreed.

On his way out, Daniel said his goodbyes to Cindy and the kittens. When Allison walked him to the front door something occurred to him.

"Are the kittens okay? I mean, from what you said it sounded like Randy really hurt them. But from what I can see, they seem fine to me."

"They appear to be. But I'm certain Cindy was convinced Randy had killed at least one of them. She had us out in the backyard looking for the other one until it got dark. And when she opened the kitchen door this morning and found them at the bottom of the steps, her surprise was genuine. She screamed so loud Ryan came running over. He was just leaving when you showed up," Allison said with a sly grin, playing to Daniel's earlier assumptions about herself and Ryan.

Daniel thought about it for a second. "Well then, they must be a lot tougher than they look," he said with a smile.

"If that's the case, then they've came to the right house," Allison replied, smiling back.

As Daniel was descending the front steps, he caught the reflection of something shining in the bushes. Realizing what it was, he chuckled, then reached out to retrieve it. It was the card he'd given Randy. He placed it back into his jacket pocket. "Nice try asshole," he said out loud, then started whistling the familiar happy-go-lucky tune and continued to the car.

Daniel followed Allison's directions and was not disappointed. Randy's car was parked on the street in front of Tony's house. Immediately, he got on the phone with Detective Bronson, the lead detective on Mark's case. After catching Bronson up on all he knew, both met at the station to prepare the necessary paperwork required to obtain a search warrant. It was critical they search Randy's belongings before he had a chance to get rid of the gun. Both knew that gun might be the only thing they had linking Randy to Mark's murder. They just hoped they could get the warrant in time

Chapter 18

By early evening Tony had long since passed out, but not Randy. His arm was throbbing. The alcohol and pot only numbed it temporarily. "Damn doctors, what do they know," Randy mumbled as he stood in Tony's bathroom, rewrapping the infected scratch with a fresh bandage. But as painful as his arm was, it was nothing compared to the storm raging in his head. Rejoining his passed-out buddy in the living room, Randy sat down on Tony's torn up old couch, cradling his arm. The images of what he saw at Allison's earlier that morning kept playing over in his mind. "Another cop!" Randy grumbled. Just like what happened years before. Another cop was moving in on his life, his woman! And just like before, was threatening to take it all away from him again. *Not this time!* "Not this time!" he said out loud.

Looking out the window, Randy noticed it was starting to get dark. A twisted smile spread across his face. He quietly stood up and walked into the bedroom to retrieve his gun. "I hope you and the brat don't have plans tonight." He secured the gun in the waistband under his shirt. Seeing Tony still crashed out, Randy grabbed Tony's car keys off the kitchen counter instead of his own. Where he was going, he wanted to make sure he wouldn't be recognized.

It was 7:30p.m. when Daniel and Detective Bronson

arrived at Tony's house. It had taken four hours to process all the necessary paperwork and get a search warrant. He was excited to see Randy's car still parked on the street, but the other car that had been in the driveway when he drove by earlier was gone. Four other patrol units joined them. After the officers took up positions around the home, Detective Bronson knocked on the front door.

"This is the Police! We have a warrant to search these premises!"

Daniel and Detective Bronson along with two of the uniformed officers stood silently on the front porch, listening for any movement coming from inside the house but heard nothing. Again, the detective knocked.

This time they heard stirring. "Hold on, I'm coming," said a heavily slurred voice. Hearing the sound of footsteps approaching, the officers prepared themselves. One never knew what to expect these days.

The door slowly opened and a sloppily dressed, disheveled portly man with a huge belly hanging out from under a heavily soiled T-shirt stood before them. What was left of his hair was hanging in his face, partly covering his eyes. Still groggy, Tony said, "What do you want?"

The detective presented him with the warrant and then pushed him aside as he and the other officers entered the house.

"We're looking for Randy Johnson, is he here?" Detective Bronson demanded.

Sobering up quickly, Tony pointed to Randy's bedroom.

Two of the uniformed officers busted in the closed door, but nobody was there. They found the duffel bag Allison described and the box, but it was empty. No gun. The officers continued looking around the room and house while Daniel and Detective Bronson returned to the front room to question Tony.

"Where is Randy Johnson?" Daniel demanded.

Tony might talk tough to Randy and his other buddies about his exploits with the police, but when confronted with a house full of police officers, he caved fast. "I don't know," he said, whimpering like a frightened child.

"His car is outside, and we know he's been staying here, now tell us where he is!" Daniel demanded. Gone was the pleasant demeanor he displayed with Allison earlier that morning. The man standing before Tony now was truly terrifying to say the least.

Again, Tony claimed not to know where Randy was, then noticed his car keys missing from the counter. He looked out the window and said in a panic, "I don't know where he is, but he has my car! It's gone!" He pointed frantically out the window at the empty driveway.

Immediately they issued an alert for Tony's faded green 2006 Ford Taurus. Officers were also warned that the suspect might be armed.

Figuring Tony would try to warn Randy with a phone call, they attempted to arrest him for possession of marijuana with the intent to distribute. Tony protested and insisted what he had was for medicinal use only and even presented medical documentation to prove it. Unfortunately for Tony, while the officers were searching for the gun, they uncovered a large stash of meth under the kitchen sink. Tony immediately denied any knowledge of the meth and insisted it must be Randy's. But it did him no good. The meth was just the excuse they needed to lock him up while they searched for Randy. The officers quickly loaded Tony into a patrol car and took him away, then closed up the house. They hoped Randy hadn't already driven by and been tipped off. Still hopeful, Detective Bronson and Daniel stayed behind in an unmarked car to stake out the premises from a position less conspicuous down the street. Daniel was disappointed, but far from ready to give up. He knew it was just a matter of time before they found Randy.

Chapter 19

Allison waved at Ryan as he pulled out of his driveway around 6:30p.m. that evening. She'd been working in the yard ever since getting back from the store with the kitten supplies. Allison didn't ask Cindy for help since she was having so much fun playing with the kittens. After all, Buddy and O were adorable. And truth be known, Allison liked working in the yard by herself. It gave her time to think and focus on the duties before her. Something about working outside helped Allison calm her mind and allowed her to escape into other tasks. After several hours, she'd amassed a huge pile of debris on the street for garbage pickup.

Noticing the large pile of yard trash, Ryan pulled his car over in front of her house and put his window down.

"Wish us luck," Ryan said, holding up his hand with his fingers crossed. This would officially be the largest venue he and the band had performed in to date. Even though Ryan made it a point to constantly stress that being a rock star was not his goal in life, he was finding he really enjoyed performing in front of live audiences. Something about it was energizing. This was also one of the main reasons he liked working in the advertising field so much. In a way, he had the opportunity to perform there too, just on a smaller stage.

"Good luck!" Allison excitedly yelled back, holding up both hands with fingers crossed.

"You've been busy," Ryan said, pointing to the large pile

of yard trash.

Allison walked toward the car, removing her gloves. "That about does it for me today. I need to get dinner started for me and the munchkin."

"Speaking of Cindy, how are the two little ones adjusting to their new home?"

"We've had a few accidents, but so far so good. Cindy is crazy about them."

Ryan lowered his head and pretended to be guilty. "I have a small confession to make... I've known she's had the kittens for a few days. I caught her playing with them on the creek bank and offered to get her the kitten food. She'd been feeding them leftovers out of your refrigerator." He looked up and shrugged while smiling.

Allison frowned, then laughed, and said, "You're forgiven."

Ryan shook his head. "I have to be honest about something else too... When Cindy said Randy tried to kill those kittens, it took everything I had not to knock his ass out right there. She sounded pretty confident about what happened. Then seeing them this morning was a real shock. I was so relieved. All night I thought about going to a pet store or a shelter to try to find her two replacements."

"I know. I think even Randy thought he'd killed them. You heard him so coldly say he took care of the problem." Allison briefly fell silent, then uttered, "monster," before continuing.

"All I know is somehow those two little cuties survived

–and I know Cindy was surprised, too. That scream this morning was 100 percent legitimate!"

"Any word from Randy?" Ryan asked, his tone more serious.

Allison shook her head no. She looked around to make sure Cindy wasn't within earshot, then bent down closer to the open window. "As you know, Daniel was here this morning. He had some interesting theories linking Randy to Mark's murder, even going so far as to speculate that Randy might have been the one who killed Mark."

"Allison…" Ryan was speechless for a moment. The significance of what she said hit him in the same way it had hit her earlier. One of the reasons she needed to get out of the house and into the yard to do something mind-numbing. A distraction to keep her from dwelling on it all day.

"Allison, if that's true, you guys need to be careful. Would you like to stay at my house to be safe? I'll give you the key right now?" Ryan offered.

"I think we'll be ok. The locks are changed. Daniel told me not to let him in under any circumstances and to call him and the police if Randy showed up at the house for any reason."

Ryan shook his head and added, "And me. Call me, too, if you need help with anything. I'd still like the opportunity to kick his ass." He smiled, trying to lighten the atmosphere.

Allison laughed. "Thank you, Ryan. Thank you for all you've done and for always being such a good friend and neighbor. It was so wrong of us to cut you off like we did, I'm so sorry for that—"

Ryan raised a hand. "No apologies necessary. I understand why you had to do it. And knowing what we know now, maybe it was a good thing for all of us that you did."

He reached out the window and took her hand. Gently squeezing it, he smiled a mischievous smile. "So, correct me if I'm wrong, but did I sense a little something between you and the detective this morning?" He raised his eyebrows a few times, grinning excitedly.

Allison pulled her hand away and lightly smacked him on the shoulder. "That's none of your business," she replied with an embarrassed grin.

"Okay, Okay. Just saying I thought I sensed a little something there..."

Allison clearly lit up when Ryan brought up Daniel.

"Way too early to tell. But one thing is for certain, I'm not blindly running into another relationship. I'm definitely going to take it slow this time."

"Good luck with that. I thought I felt some serious heat building between you and the detective..." He again raised his eyebrows up and down and threw in a wink.

"Get out of here before you're late to your own show," she said, stepping back from the car and waving him off with a gardening glove.

Ryan waved as he pulled away. Looking in the rearview mirror, he couldn't help but worry. If Randy did kill Mark, who knows what else he's capable of ...

Chapter 20

Randy returned to Allison's neighborhood a little before 10p.m. He'd taken Tony's car so he wouldn't be recognized. He parked farther down the street and around the corner next to a small private park the neighborhood sometimes used for special events. It wasn't unusual for guests of other neighbors to use this area as overflow parking. The neighborhood had an irregular shape because of the way the creek wound through it, causing the streets to be narrow, which sometimes made street parking tight.

The many large oak trees were causing the streetlights to cast huge shadows throughout the neighborhood. Concealed by the shadows, Randy reached under his seat and pulled out the gun. Out of habit, he checked the cylinder to make sure it was fully loaded. Satisfied, he flipped his wrist, snapping the cylinder back into place. When he got out of the car, he slipped the gun into his waistband and pulled his shirt down to conceal it. Again, he looked to see if anyone was around. Satisfied he was alone, Randy pulled a black ski mask over his head and then disappeared into the darkness. Using the shadows as cover, he stealthily made his way toward Allison's house on foot.

"Ok young lady, it's time to put your playmates away and get ready for bed," Allison said, walking into Cindy's room.

It had been a long day. After she returned home from the grocery store with all the items they needed for the kittens, Allison changed and committed to picking up around the yard. She knew Cindy would be more than happy to help, but instead suggested she look after the kittens since this was their first day inside the house. It also gave Allison time to process all that Daniel had told her earlier that morning.

Cindy was coloring at her desk when her mom walked over to see what she was working on. "Wow baby, these drawings are really good," Allison said, looking over Cindy's shoulder at the pictures laying next to her. They were the same ones from the classroom, but now with even more detail. One particular drawing got Allison's attention. It was a black and white cat with a police badge on its chest. Picking it up and examining it more closely, she noticed it was Mark's badge number. "And who is this handsome fellow?" Allison asked.

"That's Mr. Kitty. He's a friend." Cindy replied, still scribbling a few more details on another picture she was finishing up.

Allison knew Cindy had an active imagination and figured the large, mostly black cat with white patches on its chest and face was probably just another one of her many imaginary playmates. Allison noticed Cindy had given even more attention to the cat's eyes since the last time she saw the picture. It almost looked as if she intended for them to be glowing now. Allison admired the detail a little longer before replacing the drawing on the desk.

"Ok young lady, start finishing up so you can brush your teeth and get ready for bed. Tomorrow, you can help me with more yard work," Allison said, knowing Cindy didn't mind. She used to help her dad all the time.

"Mommy? Can the kittens sleep in here with me tonight?" Cindy asked, giving her mom the cutest pleading look, big brown eyes looking up with the pure innocence of a 7-year-old. Buddy and O were running free on the bedroom floor behind her.

Allison had long since become immune to Cindy's puppy-dog eyes, but also understood how important the kittens were to her. She smiled. "Yes, but they have to stay in their box with the cat litter. We've already had a few accidents today, let's try not to have anymore," Allison said. She picked up O and gave him a quick kiss on his head before placing him into the box. Cindy handed her mom Buddy and said, "If you kissed one goodnight you have to kiss the other one, too." Allison happily did as instructed and then placed Buddy in the box with his brother.

After Cindy brushed her teeth, Allison tucked her into bed. Allison laid with Cindy for a few minutes, but was determined not to fall asleep this time.

"I like Officer Baxter, he reminds me of Daddy," Cindy said, snuggling against her mom while cuddling with a favorite stuffed animal, a bear Mark had won for Allison at a county fair years ago. Cindy was only two years old at the time Allison gave her the bear, and she'd been sleeping with it every night since.

Allison smiled. "I like him too. He and your dad were friends when we first met."

Cindy was quiet, then said, "Thank you for letting me

keep Buddy and O."

Allison smiled and pulled Cindy close. "Just promise me you'll keep their litter box clean," Allison joked, hugging her tight.

"Mommy? Do you think Daddy is in heaven watching over us?"

Allison momentarily froze. The question was unexpected. Cindy hadn't really spoken much about her father since his death, but then again, Allison knew she was to blame for that. After Mark's death, Allison poured herself into work. Some of that was to keep busy, but mostly it was to help make ends meet. Mark's passing put a heavy financial strain on Allison, but she was determined to keep the house for Cindy's sake. Gently caressing Cindy's hair, Allison looked toward the ceiling and smiled. "Yes honey, I think he is. I think he would be very proud of you, and I especially think he would like the pictures you've drawn." She was thinking mostly about the black and white cat with the police badge.

"I do, too. I don't know how he did it, but I think he saved all of our lives last night, especially Buddy and O's."

She could tell by Cindy's tone that she was convinced of this. Allison felt an enormous amount of guilt for bringing Randy into their home and knew she'd have to live with that mistake for the rest of her life. She replayed the previous evening over in her mind. Hearing Cindy's scream and then Ryan and James showing up when they did was truly fortunate. Maybe Mark did have something to do with that as well as Cindy being rescued in the creek. Maybe he really was watching over them? Allison again looked toward the ceiling and quietly mouthed "Thank you." She gently hugged Cindy and whispered into her ear, "Your father loved you very much. I'm sure he's watching over you and will protect you and all of us to the best of his abilities. Your father was truly a good man."

Cindy hugged her mom back. She could tell her mom was becoming emotional, so she lightened the mood by recalling some funny exploits with the boys that day. They laid there talking and laughing about the kittens a little while longer. Finally, the day caught up with Cindy, and she drifted off to sleep. Allison quietly got up and turned off the small lamp on Cindy's bedside table.

"Goodnight baby. I love you," Allison said, standing in the doorway, but Cindy did not hear, she was already sound sleep. Allison quietly closed the door, leaving it just barely cracked.

Buddy and O continued to play-wrestle in the box until exhaustion set in. It had been a busy day for them, too. The inside of the house offered many new areas and textures to explore. Tired, the boys curled up on a soft towel next to each other and drifted off to sleep, safe at last from all the dangers of the outside world.

It had been an especially long day for Allison. Daniel had given her a lot to think about. The thought that Randy might have had something to do with Mark's death was frightening. She didn't want to believe it, but the more she thought about it, the more she realized it was a very real possibility. After seeing Randy just standing there that day on the creek bank and then seeing the same look on his face when he chased Cindy up the path, she was more terrified of him than ever. Monster was the word that kept coming to mind. "Monster" she said, out loud.

Noticing the time, Allison decided to call it a night. She briefly thought about Ryan and hoped his show was going well. She'd like to start going to the shows again, but clearly this was not the night to do so. She smiled when thinking about maybe going with Daniel at some future date. His wanting to kiss her that morning was not missed. She liked Daniel, but she was determined she wasn't going to rush into anything this time. Still, the thought of going on a date with him made her smile. Before she knew it, she was gleefully humming while walking around the house, turning off lights.

Masked and dressed in black, Randy kept to the shadows as he quietly made his way through the neighborhood to Allison's house. It was a little past 10p.m. when he crept up the driveway and disappeared into a thick hedge. Hiding in bushes next to the front steps, Randy carefully peered through the dining room windows, trying to figure out where Allison was inside the house, but saw no sign of her. Staying concealed in the bushes along the house, he crept up the driveway toward the backyard gate entrance. This was the same gate Ryan and James used the previous night. Randy paused on the driveway to check Ryan's house. It looked dark and then he remembered the band had a show that night. Feeling relieved

Ryan wasn't home, Randy continued to the back gate. Once there, he quietly lifted the latch and went through.

As Randy was trying to gently close the gate, the wind caught it and slammed it shut. Randy froze. He stood hidden in the shadows, listening to see if anyone had heard the sound. After a few seconds, he reasoned it was safe and quietly moved toward the back door. He tried his key, but it didn't work. Randy knew Allison would eventually have the locks changed, he just didn't think she'd have done it so soon. He even tried the dog door to see if it was open, but it too was locked.

Randy continued around the house, now freer in his movements since he felt more concealed by the darkness and heavily overgrown vegetation in the back yard. Making his way to Cindy's bedroom window, he paused. The curtains were drawn but he could just barely hear voices. Noticing a tiny slit in the curtains, he looked in. Allison was laying on the bed with Cindy. A twisted smile spread across his face. If he wanted to get inside, now would be his best chance. He quickly made his way around the house to the master bathroom window.

Lying in a lounge chair on Ryan's pool deck, Tor was grooming himself when he heard the gate slam shut. Looking in the direction of Cindy's house, he froze. A gentle breeze was rustling the leaves in the trees above him, but otherwise the night was quiet. Tor sniffed the air. Catching the faint hint of something familiar, he hopped down off the chair and moved closer to the edge of the deck. Standing as still as a statue, he again smelled the night air. This time the scent was stronger. Tor's eyes immediately ignited into a blazing yellow-green glow. Randy was back. In a flash he leapt from the deck into the yard and shot off toward the gap in the fence.

Randy quietly crept around the house until he reached the master bathroom window. Though the house was only one story, it was still built about three feet off the ground, placing the window at eye level. The bathroom was dark, but light from the bedroom illuminated it enough to see inside. The master bedroom and bathroom were in the far back corner of the house. Thanks to the dense vegetation and darkness, Randy felt confident he wouldn't be detected by the neighbors. Slowly, he pushed up on the window. It moved. Again, another sinister smile spread across his lips. Quietly, he continued pushing up on the window until it was open enough for him to climb through. Unseen by Ryan and James, he'd unlocked the window the night before when he was collecting his personal items from the bathroom.

When Tor reached the back door, Randy's scent was strong. Following it, he continued around the house. At Cindy's bedroom window it was overpowering. Tor continued racing around the house following the scent. He rounded the back corner just in time to see Randy's boot disappearing inside the partly opened bathroom window and then it closed.

Tor jumped to the window ledge, but it was too late. Looking through the window, he just caught a glimpse of Randy's dark figure exiting the bathroom. Randy was inside the house.

Chapter 21

Parked down the street from Tony's, Daniel and Detective Bronson were still hopeful Randy had not spotted their earlier raid on the house and would soon be returning home. To pass the time, Daniel and Bronson discussed the new information he'd found out about Randy over the past few days.

"If Randy is indeed our man, he's a very disturbed individual. To kill his ex-girlfriend's husband and then move into his home in an attempt to take over his life is pretty damn twisted," Bronson remarked.

"Extremely. But then something must not have been working for him. From what Allison said, he changed soon after moving in. Cindy claimed he boasted about killing the family dog and throwing its body into the creek. And Allison and her neighbor are confident Randy was just standing by and watching from the creek bank as the little girl was drowning," Daniel added.

"He became resentful," Bronson said.

Daniel nodded his head and looked out the window before continuing. "Randy moved in, but the longer he lived there the more resentful he became. Looking around, everything reminded him of Mark. He might have killed the man, but not the memory. Then, as time went on, he started feeling trapped in a prison of his own making."

"Yes, and in a warped attempt to escape, he started

removing all of the reminders of Mark that he could. Poor little Cindy. As Mark's daughter, she was probably the biggest and most irritating reminder. After all, she's a product of their actual physical union and a constant visual reminder of Allison being with another man. I'm confident his jealousy toward Cindy has been off the chart for some time. I bet the only reason Cindy didn't have an accident sooner was because he got some kind of sick satisfaction out of harassing and hurting her. It was his twisted way of displacing his hatred for Mark onto her," Bronson speculated.

Daniel noticed the time. It was a little past 10p.m. He wasn't losing hope, but he was becoming more anxious. Not knowing where Randy was and why he'd taken Tony's car was troubling him. *"Why take Tony's car?"* he thought, nervously tapping the bottom of his seat and looking toward Tony's house.

Chapter 22

After leaving Cindy's room, Allison headed to bed. The morning started off exciting enough with the discovery of the kittens. Then Daniel's visit and the bombshell of suspicion he shared with her regarding Randy and his possible involvement in Mark's murder only added that much more to the mix. Needing to process all Daniel told her, Allison threw herself into cleaning up around the yard. The task was monumental, and she knew to really get a handle on all that needed to be done, she'd have to call a professional landscaper. As she walked around the house turning off lights, she decided to catch Ryan at some point the next day and ask if he thought his landscaping crew would be interested in tackling the out-of-control mess of a yard. Maybe even see if he could recommend someone to help resurrect the long-neglected pool, too.

Standing in the den, Allison smiled. She remembered how cozy she, Mark and Cindy would get on the couch as they enjoyed their Saturday night movie time together. Looking around the room, she realized it had been some time since she cozied up on the couch and watched anything in the room. Randy had taken it over for himself. She and Cindy rarely ventured in anymore. But standing there now, she remembered the good times the three of them shared watching movies and eating popcorn together before Mark's death.

Focusing on the coffee table in front of the couch, Allison sighed. The finish on the top of the table had been badly damaged by Randy's numerous beer bottle water rings. It was a beautiful table at one time. She and Mark had found it in a small antique store in Highlands, North Carolina. Seeing it now angered her. The utter disrespect Randy showed for the house and her belongings was sickening. What did she ever see in him? She ran her fingers over the damaged surface. Shaking her head, Allison patted the table. "Another thing I need to have repaired," she said out loud.

Fortunately, the table could be repaired or replaced. Briefly thinking about Cindy in the creek, she became emotional.

"But some things can't be," she again said out loud to the empty room.

Randy was clearly a mistake and now knowing what Daniel had told her, she felt lucky she and Cindy had gotten away from him when they did. She turned off the two end table lights in the den and then made her way into the kitchen to do a nightly check and shut down in there as well.

When Allison reached the back door, she noticed the top lock had already been locked but the key was missing. Usually, they left the key in the lock during the day and used it as a deadbolt. But in the evenings, they removed it and placed it on the counter by the sink. The key was gone, but fortunately the door was already locked. Allison figured Cindy must have locked it and probably forgot to leave the key on the counter. She didn't think much of it since Cindy had been trying to be helpful all day. But it did make her pause to think. Cindy wasn't tall enough to reach the top lock without the small kitchen stepping stool. Looking around, Allison noticed the stool was still in the corner where it's always kept. She didn't remember Cindy coming into the kitchen either, but then again, it had been a long day. She figured maybe Cindy locked it after she came in from the yard and was showering. Knowing Cindy was fast asleep, Allison decided it could wait until the morning. After all, it had to be there somewhere, she thought.

Allison turned on a small night light under the microwave for Cindy in case she got up during the night and needed something from the kitchen. She then turned off the main overhead kitchen light and headed toward her room. It had been a long day, and she was looking forward to climbing into bed and calling it a night.

The hallway was dark, but the light from her bedroom at the end of the hall illuminated it enough to see where she was going. As she walked by the archway to the living room, a hand suddenly appeared out of the darkness and forcefully pressed against her mouth. Then a strong arm wrapped around her waist and violently yanked her into the dark room. Suddenly, there was an explosion of pain on the right side of her head as a fist repeatedly landed blow after blow against her right temple, followed by repeated abdominal blows, knocking the wind out of her.

Allison tried gasping for breath, but the gloved hand remained firmly over her mouth as more violent blows followed. She desperately grabbed at the gloved hand while kicking wildly, but only managed to knock over a small table in the darkened room. It was no use. With every blow, she felt the strength rapidly draining from her body.

Badly beaten and on the verge of passing out, Allison's body went limp. Suddenly a rag was forced into her mouth. She then heard the sound of duct tape being ripped from a roll. Dazed and confused, she felt the tape being wrapped around her mouth and head in repeated loops. Then, all of a sudden, she was flipped over on her stomach, and her arms were pulled behind her. Again, the sound of the duct tape before she felt her wrists being taped together in repeated tight loops. She was then picked up and carried farther into the living room where she was forcefully thrown to the floor.

Frozen with fear, Allison could hear footsteps moving around the room, then heard the curtains being shut. For a second, there was an eerie silence. Terrified, all she could do was wait, listening for any sound in the darkness. Suddenly, a light was switched on behind her. Hearing footsteps approach, Allison cringed, expecting another blow. But instead, she heard a frighteningly familiar voice.

"Did you miss me?" Randy asked, removing his mask and pulling her up by her hair to face him.

Hearing something, Cindy woke up. She thought the kittens were probably playing in their box, but when she looked in, she realized they were fast asleep. She laid back down in her bed, listening. Again, she heard movement in the house. It sounded like dull thumps, but she couldn't tell what it was. The sounds were scary. Quietly, she got up and stood by her cracked bedroom door, listening. Everything was quiet. Then she heard a hard, loud thud, like something heavy was dropped on the floor. A few seconds later a light came on in the living room. Cindy's room was midway down the hall, closer to the kitchen than Allison's room. Standing behind her cracked door, she listened intently. Hearing a chillingly familiar voice, she knew immediately that Randy was in the house.

∽◦≪

Realizing he couldn't get in through the closed bathroom window, Tor franticly ran around the house looking for another way in but had no luck. Noticing the dog door, he tried pushing on it, but it wouldn't budge. Tor could sense trouble inside the house, but for the moment he was powerless to do anything about it.

∽◦≪

Cindy quietly slid the box with Buddy and O in it into her closet and covered it with a towel and other clothes before shutting the door. Randy already tried to kill the kittens once; she was sure he'd try again if he found them in the house. She then returned to the door and quietly opened it. She could hear Randy's voice in the living room, so she carefully crept down the hall to see what was going on. She heard him talking, but thought it strange that she didn't hear her mom talking back. When she rounded the corner, she realized why. Seeing her mom laying on the floor made her heart skip a beat. Randy was kneeling next to her with his back toward the dark hallway. Cindy was frozen with fear. But what he said next shocked her to her core.

Still kneeling beside Allison, Randy was drunk with power. He taunted her by slapping her face and head as he spoke.

"I'm not going to let another cop or some wanna-be rock star take what's mine, not like last time. Your precious Mark took you away from me once, I'll be damned if I'm going to let it happen again. If I can't have you, nobody can," Randy hissed in her ear.

Allison was completely helpless. Bound and gagged and in excruciating pain, she was powerless to do anything. Her face was bloody and starting to swell. All she could do was lay there and listen to Randy's gloating.

Pulling the gun from his waistband, he pressed it to the side of Allison's head. "By the way, I thought you might like to know this is the same gun I used to kill your beloved Mark. Yes, it was me, I'm the one who shot him," Randy said, pressing the gun harder into the side of her head. "I knew he was on duty that evening and most likely would be the one to respond to the call since the construction site was on his way home. I shot him once in the stomach which brought him to his knees. Then I made sure he got a good look at me before I unloaded the next shot right into his head, just like I'm going to do to you." Randy again pulled her up by the hair to face him. He wanted to see her face when she learned he was the one who killed Mark.

A single tear rolled down Allison's swollen cheek but otherwise she showed no emotion. Irritated, Randy pushed her head forcefully back to the floor, then continued to rant.

"But before I use this gun on you, I'm going to get your brat and put one in her head right in front of you. Since she misses her daddy so much, I'll send her to him."

Allison screamed through the tape and desperately struggled to get free with what strength she had left, but it was to no avail. She was helpless. Realizing there was no escape, she burst into tears. Knowing he'd broken her, Randy laughed and watched Allison break down before him.

Cindy heard everything Randy said. She knew if she and her mom had any chance of surviving this maniac, it would be up to her. Quietly, she snuck back down the hall and into the kitchen where she called 911 on the landline phone just like her mom showed her how to do days before. She quietly whispered to the operator her name and address as well as her mom and Randy's name. She then told them what he said about killing her father and was planning on killing her and her mom next. She pleaded for them to get there as soon as possible. The 911 operator asked Cindy if he was armed and she said he was and tried to describe the gun. The operator knew time was critical. Keeping Cindy on the line, the operator got another 911 operator to help get the information out. In a matter of seconds, units were converging on the house from across the area.

Suddenly Randy shouted at the top of his lungs, "Wake up brat, you're next!" He was so loud even the 911 operator could hear him.

"Hide Honey, if you can, hide! The police are on their way," the operator shouted frantically into the phone.

Cindy quickly hung up and ran for the back door. Realizing it was locked, she looked for the key but didn't see it on the counter. Then she noticed Biscuit's dog door.

⤜⤏

Randy busted into Cindy's room and flipped on the light, but she was gone. He threw open the closet doors, but nothing. He knew she had to be in the house somewhere because he'd locked the back and front doors with the key. The French doors in the master bedroom were bolted shut and he knew she couldn't reach the top bolt. He'd even wedged a screwdriver in the track of the sliding doors in the den so they couldn't be opened.

"Come out, come out, where ever you are, brat. You and I have some unfinished business," Randy shouted, stomping down the hall, making his way toward the kitchen.

Cindy quickly unlocked the dog door and started climbing through. To her surprise, Tor was standing at the bottom of the steps. The door was smaller than she was, but she was still managing to squeeze through it. Her head and shoulders were just through when she felt a tight grip on her left foot. Cindy again screamed a blood-curdling scream. Tor's eyes ignited in a fiery yellow-green glow. Screaming and kicking, Cindy fought with everything she had to get free, but it was no use. Randy had ahold of her and was pulling her back through the dog door. She tried to hold on, but he kicked and stomped on her stomach. Winded, and her tiny body screaming in pain, Cindy's strength finally gave out as Randy pulled her back inside the house.

Managing one last burst of energy, Cindy was able to kick free of Randy's grip. Desperately looking for an escape, she ran down the hall. But it was no use, Randy was right behind her. Grabbing her by the back of her pajamas, he lifted her off her feet and carried her back to the living room where he forcefully threw her against the marble fireplace hearth. Striking it hard with her head, she was knocked unconscious. Allison again screamed, but it did no good. Randy casually walked into the living room and kicked Cindy hard in the side. There was no response.

"Maybe I won't need to waste a bullet on her after all," he said, looking back at Allison.

༺❧

Daniel and Detective Bronson shot bolt upright in their seats when they heard the call over the radio. Daniel quickly responded to the dispatcher and told her they were on their way. As Detective Bronson drove, the dispatcher filled them in on the call from Cindy. Racing across town, they hoped they weren't too late.

༺❧

Hearing the commotion in the kitchen, Tor could hear Randy chasing Cindy. He quickly ran up the steps and again pushed on the dog door. This time it moved. He pushed his way inside and disappeared into the house.

Chapter 23

Allison was crying hysterically. Bound and gagged, there was nothing she could do but look at Cindy's motionless body lying against the hearth.

Randy stood over Allison, laughing, and then he picked her up by the tape around her wrists. "We still have a little time, how about one more ride for old times' sake?" he said, yanking her up from the floor. But just as he did, the front curtains suddenly lit up. Light was pouring onto the house. Blue lights were flashing outside. He threw Allison down on the floor, hard. The impact knocked her out. Randy ran to the front window and carefully looked out the curtains. Two police cars were parked in the street using their spotlights to illuminate the front of the house. Randy could see the officers standing beside their cars.

"Randy Johnson. This is the Police. Come out with your hands up," one officer ordered over a megaphone.

Randy used his gun to smash out one of the living room windows, then shouted, "Stay back! Don't try to come in or I'll kill them. I swear I will!" He yanked the curtain closed and jumped back from the window. He quickly turned off the living room light. Noticing more light coming from the hall and master bedroom, he hurried out of the living room to extinguish those lights as well.

Bursting into Allison's bedroom, Randy frantically

looked around. Noticing a bedside table light on, he quickly ran over and turned it off. The room was mostly dark but the powerful lights the police had aimed at the front of the house illuminated it enough to see.

When Randy turned around, Tor was standing on the bed. His eyes ignited in a blinding yellow-green glow. Ears back, teeth bared, he growled ferociously. Still holding the gun, Randy raised his arm and fired, but it was too late. Tor pounced and landed another blow, knocking the gun away and sending Randy flying across the room. It was like he'd been hit with another sledgehammer. Shaking it off, Randy staggered to his feet and retrieved the gun. Dazed, he looked at the bed, but Tor was gone.

"Shots fired! Shots fired!" another officer shouted into the radio.

At the same time Daniel and Detective Bronson came racing down the street. Daniel was out of the car before it stopped. "What's the situation?" he asked as he hurriedly joined the officers behind the nearest police cruiser.

"We know the suspect is armed and has two hostages. We just heard a gunshot seconds before you arrived. The SWAT team is on its way," the officer informed him.

Still standing in the bedroom, Randy tried to shake off

the hit when he heard Tor growl again. The cat was still in the room. Randy froze. He looked around, but could see no sign of him. The room was quiet. Then Tor growled again, this time much louder.

"Where are you?" Randy shouted and wildly kicked the bed in panicked desperation.

Tor shot out of the room and down the hall.

Randy just barely made out Tor's outline as he ran from the room. Again, he fired, but to no avail, Tor was already gone. Randy attempted to follow, but his legs felt heavy, and his movements were slow. Something was wrong. Why was he so drained? He desperately tried to shake it off. "What have you done to me?" Randy hysterically shouted, clumsily chasing after the cat.

❦

"Shots fired! Shots fired!" the officer again shouted over the radio. "Where the hell is that SWAT team?"

Daniel grabbed the megaphone. "Randy Johnson!" he desperately called out. But nothing. No response from the house.

❦

Tor ran to the den and growled, then to the kitchen, growling again. He was toying with Randy.

"Where are you cat?" Randy shouted hysterically into the darkness.

Tor ran from the dimly lit kitchen into the dining room and then the foyer. Randy tried to keep up but his arm was throbbing, and his legs were so heavy he was having trouble walking. When he reached the foyer, he paused. Both sides of the front door were bordered by narrow glass windows. He wasn't sure who was out there and didn't want to give anyone a clear target.

Tor ran into the living room and growled again from the shadows. Hearing him, Randy went back around through the dining room and kitchen, then came back up the hall and entered the living room.

When Randy rounded the corner, he was face-to-face with Tor and didn't know it. Tor had jumped on top of a low curio cabinet and was waiting in the darkness. Tor's eyes ignited. Randy tried to raise his arm with the gun in it, but it felt heavy and protested with pain. Teeth bared, Tor hissed and leapt on Randy. The gun fired again directly into the floor. Ears back and eyes glowing as bright as the sun, Tor growled viciously while sinking his claws deep into Randy's chest and shoulder.

Randy was instantly paralyzed. Tor's eyes burned brightly as he consumed all of Randy's life force in a matter of seconds, causing his body to collapse into a crumpled heap on the hallway floor.

"Shots fired!" was again screamed into the radio.

"A third shot," Daniel said, looking at Detective Bronson.

"One for Cindy, one for Allison, and one for himself."

"We don't know that," Bronson said, clearly irritated too. "Where the hell is the goddamn SWAT team?"

The gunshot startled Cindy awake. Her eyes opened just in time to see Tor attacking Randy. Though the image was blurry, the yellow-green brightness illuminated the room. Tor jumped off Randy's lifeless body and landed close to Cindy.

"Mr. Kitty," she said in a raspy voice. She was struggling to breathe because of a collapsed lung.

Tor trotted over to her and put his cold wet nose right against Cindy's. He could tell she was in bad shape. Her concussion was causing her to drift in and out of consciousness. Randy's violent attack left her with multiple broken ribs, a collapsed lung and a ruptured spleen.

Slowly, Tor's eyes began to glow. Cindy could feel the soothing yellow-green light becoming stronger. Her breathing was difficult, but with each ragged breath she was able to take in more of his healing energy.

Immediately Cindy felt the pain easing. She could feel the same soothing warmth spreading to her head, chest, and stomach. The more energy she took in, the better her breathing was becoming. The pain was slowly subsiding. Cindy was a much larger lifeform, so Tor could only do so much, but somehow Cindy's body was able to focus the energy where it was needed most. The more energy she took in, the better she was feeling.

Allison coughed and then moaned as she started to regain consciousness. Hearing Allison, Tor's eyes returned to normal. Because of his size, he didn't have the ability to repair all of Cindy's physical damage, but he was able to repair most of it.

Feeling a little better, Cindy forced a smile. "Thank you, Mr. Kitty," she said with a raspy voice, straining to force the words out. Tor again flashed his eyes and gently rubbed against her. Then his eyes glowed softly and as with the kittens, in a few seconds Cindy laid her head down and fell back to sleep, her breathing much improved.

Chapter 24

In all fairness, it had only been a little over ten minutes since the request for SWAT was sent. The situation was fluid. At the moment, all they knew was what Cindy told the 911 operator. The first officers on the scene attempted to contact the suspect, but he warned them away. All attempts to reach Randy after that were met with silence. Knowing he had hostages, the police called for a hostage negotiator as well as SWAT for backup. But the situation was evolving fast. After hearing the first two gunshots, the police closed off the street and evacuated nearby homes. Moments after the third shot was fired, SWAT arrived on the scene.

After trying repeatedly to contact anyone in the house, the tactical team decided to move in, three team members per entry location. One group would take the front door, another the kitchen door, and another the bedroom French doors. The sliders off the den would be monitored, but not used as an entry point at that time. When all the teams were in place, a signal would be given for a coordinated entry.

Standing next to Cindy, Tor sensed movement around the house and quickly retreated to the dog door in the kitchen. Shooting through the door, Tor startled the backdoor SWAT team as he burst out and ran off into the darkness.

The teams listened in as the team leader counted down to entry. Suddenly, as per procedure, the spotlights bathing the house in bright light were turned off. In one swift motion all three teams burst through their assigned entryways. All members were wearing night-vision goggles and had a clear picture of the darkened interior. Team three quickly cleared the bedroom and started moving toward the other two teams, clearing rooms as they moved. Team two cleared the kitchen and den and just started into the hall when the team leader announced they had a body in the hall. Team one entered the front door, and a team member quickly cleared the dining room. The other two entered the living room. "We have bodies here. I repeat, we have bodies here."

Daniel and Bronson were listening from the trailer the SWAT team used as its mobile command center.

"We're too late," Daniel said out loud.

Detective Bronson remained silent, but put his hand on Daniel's shoulder.

Allison was awake and trying desperately to scream for help. Hearing her and seeing the movement, a SWAT member said over the radio, "We have a survivor. An adult woman, bound and gagged."

Seeing Cindy lying next to the fireplace, another member checked on her. "She's alive!" he shouted. "We have a second survivor, a little girl. She's alive, but unconscious."

Daniel's face lit up. He took off out of the command truck and ran toward the house. The paramedics were just ahead, standing by for the all-clear to enter.

Team two had not reported back yet. They were assessing Randy's lifeless body. He was lying on his side in the hallway entrance to the living room. His eyes were open, but his face was frozen in a horrific expression of fear. Still holding the gun, the team approached with caution. Checking for vitals, he was confirmed dead at the scene.

"Have you ever seen anything like that?" asked one of the SWAT members.

"No. It looks like he was frightened to death," the team leader answered back.

The SWAT teams quickly secured the scene and requested medical assistance for Allison and Cindy. Daniel hurriedly followed the paramedics into the house. Allison had already been untied and was frantically trying to get to Cindy when Daniel and the paramedics entered the living room. He ran to her in an attempt to calm her.

"She's going to be okay," Daniel kept repeating, but Allison was desperate to get to her daughter. He gently restrained her so the paramedics could see to Cindy.

"Mommy..." Cindy said in a raspy voice.

Badly broken and wracked with pain herself, Allison pushed away from Daniel and dove to the floor beside Cindy. Careful not to move her, she took her small hand and gently stroked it. "It's okay baby, it's all going to be okay," she said, tears spilled down her face. The paramedics gave them a moment before returning to their duties.

"Ma'am, we need to get the two of you to the hospital," one of the paramedics said, trying to politely regain control over the situation.

Daniel kneeled beside Allison and smiled at Cindy.

"Officer Baxter, the kittens are in my closet. Please look after them for me." Her big brown eyes melted his heart.

"Of course I will. I'll take good care of them until you and your mommy are better."

Cindy smiled back. Knowing the kittens would be ok gave her a sense of peace.

Not knowing the full extent of Cindy's injuries, they secured her to a board and carefully loaded it onto a gurney to be wheeled to the ambulance waiting outside.

Allison insisted on walking beside the gurney as they wheeled Cindy out. Her face was bloody and swollen, her body was screaming in pain, but she refused to let go of Cindy's hand. Daniel walked beside Allison, helping to hold her up. Everyone was aware that trying to separate the two would be futile. Once they reached the ambulance, the paramedics were finally able to get Allison to let go of Cindy so they could load her inside.

Allison turned to Daniel and tried to manage a smile.

"I'm sure I look awful," she said, looking away.

He slowly and carefully turned her head back facing him. "Not in my eyes," he said, then softly kissed her on her lips. Badly bruised and beaten, she looked as beautiful as ever to Daniel. Allison squeezed his hand and tried to smile. "Thank you," she said, but before she could say anything else, he cut her off.

"Now let's get the two of you to the hospital," Daniel insisted in a more official tone.

The paramedics helped Allison into the ambulance and quickly secured her in a second gurney. Daniel could see her reach out and take Cindy's hand as the doors to the ambulance were closing.

Concerned about internal injuries, the ambulance raced off into the night with lights flashing and sirens blaring.

Detective Bronson joined Daniel on the street. "They're going to be okay. Why don't you go to the hospital and take their statements when they're ready, I'll wrap up here," Bronson offered, knowing that's where he wanted to be anyway.

Daniel shook his head silently then said, "I have kittens to find first, then I just might do that."

❧

After Daniel left, Detective Bronson and Frank Cohens from the Medical Examiner's Office stood over Randy's lifeless body. The bandage on Randy's arm had come undone and the wound was visible.

"Look at his face, Frank, have you ever seen an expression like that?"

Pausing for a long time before answering, Frank shook his head. "No. He looks terrified, like he saw something that frightened him to death." Frank then pointed to the arm. "It's possible that infection had something to do with his death. By the looks of it, it might have caused him to have some kind of heart failure. We'll know more once we do an autopsy. Whatever happened to him, it wasn't pleasant, that's for sure."

Chapter 25

Ryan was still brimming with excitement as he drove home from the show in the early hours of the morning. The venue was the largest they'd performed in to date. Easily three thousand people were in attendance, and they were later told hundreds more had to be turned away at the door because the building had reached maximum occupancy as per the fire code. When the curtain opened, Ryan, James and the rest of the band were dumbstruck as they looked out at what appeared to be an endless sea of people gathered before them. Feeding off the crowd's energy, the band exploded to life, giving one of their best performances ever. Ryan was a natural-born showman. He and the band were having fun, and it showed. Each song surpassed the last in its enthusiasm, whipping the crowd into an excited frenzy. For an hour and thirty minutes they dominated the stage, performing as well as any professional band. After the show, the band and concert organizers were discussing the possibility of finding a larger outdoor venue for their next performance. Rock star was not the life Ryan ever envisioned for himself, but at the moment, it felt pretty damn good being one.

Despite the obvious success of the show, the evening did not conclude in its typical fashion for Ryan. Usually, he would attend various after parties where he almost always found a beautiful companion to escort him home for the evening. But not this night. For some reason, about midway through the show, he started getting a feeling that something was going on with Allison and Cindy. Random images of them kept appearing in his thoughts. It wasn't enough to throw him off his performance, but clearly, they were on his mind for some reason. He'd hoped that Allison and Daniel could come to the show, but he understood because of the recent issues with Randy, that the timing was not the best at the moment.

After the show and helping break down and load their equipment into the rented truck, Ryan congratulated his bandmates and all who'd helped make the evening such a huge success. He even promised to throw a celebratory party at his home in the near future in honor of the evening. Quietly, he told James of his concerns for Allison and Cindy. James understood. After all, he was there and saw the look on Randy's face for himself. James could tell it wasn't over for Randy, not by a long shot.

Still thinking about the show, Ryan drove down the deserted boulevard on his way home. It was late and the road was completely free of other vehicles. Suddenly, out of nowhere, a grey streak flew in front of his car. Briefly exposed by the headlights, he could see it was an owl. He attempted to brake, but it was too late. Hearing a dull thump come from his right front bumper, he knew he'd struck the animal. Looking in the rearview mirror, he saw a small clump of feathers illuminated by an overhead streetlight roll into the gutter just to the side of the road. Immediately, he turned the car around. Ryan might come off as an intimidating figure to those who don't know him, but the reality is, he's a softy when it came to animals. Unknown to many, he often contributed anonymously to local animal shelters and other animal rescue groups around town.

Ryan parked his car on the roadside and walked along the gutter, looking for the injured animal. After walking a short distance, he found what he was looking for, a small owl. Illuminated by his car's headlights, the owl appeared alert as it stood in the gutter watching him approach. Other than a sagging wing, the bird seemed okay.

Trying not to upset the animal, Ryan slowly squatted down, blocking some of the light coming from his car's headlights. Not thinking, he put his left hand in front of the bird and used the other to gently nudge it onto his hand. The bird was remarkably compliant. But once it was standing completely on his hand, it suddenly clamped down with both feet on his left ring finger. The pressure was like a vice grip. The owl wasn't frightened or attempting to harm Ryan, it tightened its grip more for stability. But to Ryan, the pain was intense. He immediately realized the error in his plan. Owls kill with their talons and have incredible strength. Ryan sucked up the pain and slowly pulled his left hand to his stomach and put his right on the bird's chest to stabilize it as he walked back to the car.

After carefully getting back in to the car, he awkwardly reached over and closed the driver's door with his right hand. Realizing the bird might want to exit at any minute, Ryan opened the sunroof and put down the windows just in case. Fortunately, his house was only a few minutes away. He knew he had some old birdcages in the garage and figured he'd use one of them to keep the owl in until he could get it to a shelter in the morning —if he could get it off his finger, that is.

As Ryan drove, the owl remained unusually calm. It

casually looked around the car and occasionally up at him. The pressure on his finger was excruciating, but he endured.

Suddenly exhausted and preoccupied by thoughts of how he was going to get the bird off his finger, Ryan drove past Allison's house and parked in the driveway, not noticing the police tape wrapped around her darkened front porch. Allison's house being dark at this time of night didn't arouse much suspicion either, since it was so late.

Ryan felt extremely tired all of a sudden. After picking up the owl, his energy level had suddenly crashed. Gone was the euphoric high he'd been riding since the show. He was now doing all he could just to stay awake on the quick drive home. Noticing the time, Ryan opened the car door, but before he could get out was overcome by a wave of fatigue. Suddenly his eyelids felt like they weighed a hundred pounds. Seeing the small owl calmly staring up at him was the last thing he saw before darkness closed in. Overcome by exhaustion, Ryan passed out, slumped over in the driver's seat.

The owl stared up at Ryan's motionless body for a few more minutes until it was satisfied he was safely incapacitated, then it shut its eyes. When it opened them again, they were glowing a soft blue-white glow that gradually grew in intensity. Slowly, the owl was draining energy from Ryan and transferring it to its broken wing. It was a slow process, nothing like what Tor did to Randy. This was intentional and deliberately controlled.

A short time later, Tor happened on Ryan's parked car in the driveway. He'd taken refuge in Ryan's backyard when SWAT raided Cindy's house. After the police left, he ventured out to do his nightly hunting. He did the bulk of his hunting along the creek bank before eventually making his way around to the front of the houses facing the street. As Tor walked up Ryan's driveway, he noticed the parked car with the open door and approached with caution.

Taking in the scene, Tor froze. The owl locked eyes on him. Tor's eyes began to glow. The owl returned the gesture. Realizing Ryan was passed out, Tor slowly advanced, stepping up on the edge of the car. He put a paw on Ryan's leg and his eyes glowed hotter. The owl physically pressed back against Ryan's stomach, its eyes glowing more intense as well. Tor's eyes ignited even brighter. An energy tug-of-war of sorts was taking place. Then, all of a sudden, Ryan stirred. He was starting to wake up. Tor had forced enough energy into Ryan to wake him. Seeing Ryan move, Tor withdrew his paw and disappeared under the car. The owl's blue-white glowing eyes quickly extinguished and went back to normal.

When Ryan came to, he looked down at the small owl.

"Ok my extremely strong little friend, let's see if we can find you a place to stay for the night."

Ryan got out of the car, being careful not to disturb the owl. When he stood, he felt the owl move. Ryan stood still. The owl checked one wing by fully extending it, then the other. Satisfied, the little bird looked up at Ryan. Briefly, they held eye contact, then the owl leapt off his hand and flew away into the darkness.

Immediately, Ryan felt relief and shook his hand. It felt good having his hand back. Then out of nowhere, he heard a loud rumble of thunder. He knew some storms had been forecasted for the evening, so he closed the car's roof and windows and made his way to the front door. He figured he'd put the car in the garage in the morning. For some reason he felt strangely energized and hungry. When he reached the front door, Tor jumped up on to the porch to greet him.

"Well, hello there. And where did you come from?" Ryan asked, reaching down to pet the extremely friendly cat. Tor purred loudly while rubbing against Ryan's legs and excitedly head-butting his hand as Ryan continued to pet him affectionately.

Laughing at the cat's excitement, Ryan couldn't help but notice how much he looked like the cat that hung out with him and the band the nights they rehearsed at the warehouse complex in the downtown Springfield neighborhood. Wondering if it could possibly be the same cat, he looked for the black collar and brass nametag but saw nothing. Still petting him he said, "You look just like a cat I know. His name is Tor. I swear you two could be twins." Then out of nowhere, lightning flashed, and another thunder clap boomed out almost directly over the house. Simultaneously, heavy rain started pouring from the sky.

Feeling a strange familiarity with the excited cat, Ryan looked down and said, "I'm sure you don't want to be out in this tonight. You're welcome to come inside if you want. I'll see what I can find for us to eat, I'm starved for some reason." When he opened the door, Tor shot inside with no hesitation. Ryan laughed. "Well then, make yourself at home."

Chapter 26

Still feeling energized, Ryan woke early for his morning run. Just as he was leaving the driveway, he noticed the police tape strung around the columns across Allison's front porch. He stopped abruptly in the street to take in the sight. "What the hell..." He reached for his cell phone.

"You missed all the excitement last night," said a voice from behind him.

It was a neighbor taking her dog for an early morning walk.

"What happened?"

"The boyfriend broke in and held Allison and Cindy hostage. The police and SWAT arrived and there was a brief standoff. They evacuated everyone in the surrounding homes and made us stay behind a barricade farther down the road. I didn't even have time to get Frankie here," she said patting the dog's head. "They rushed us all out of our houses so fast–"

"Are Allison and Cindy okay?" Ryan asked, cutting her off.

A little startled by his abrupt question, the neighbor skipped the more colorful commentary. "Yes, I think so. Allison walked out of the house next to the gurney the paramedics had Cindy on. They say she was pretty badly beaten up. After the paramedics loaded them into the ambulance, they were rushed away to the hospital. But not the boyfriend, they said he died at the scene. Something about an infection or a fatal heart attack."

"Thank you," Ryan said, backing away and quickly running back toward his house to change. He was relieved to know they were still alive.

Fifteen minutes later, Ryan was pulling into the hospital parking garage. During the show he sensed something was wrong, but after hitting the owl, he got sidetracked. After parking, Ryan quickly made his way into the hospital in pursuit of Allison and Cindy.

Allison was awake and sitting up in bed when Ryan entered her room. They had just delivered breakfast. Her head was partly wrapped in a bandage. She had two black eyes, a broken nose and her right cheek bone was broken, along with multiple broken ribs and a concussion. The concussion was the primary concern and the main reason they wanted to keep her at the hospital overnight for observation. Fortunately, none of the other injuries were considered life-threatening, but all were painful and didn't allow her to get much sleep.

"Ryan!" she said excitedly as he burst through the door.

Her appearance momentarily stopped him in his tracks. It was obvious from his expression that she looked rough.

"That bad, huh?" Allison asked, trying to lighten the mood.

Immediately Ryan caught himself and smiled. "Naw, not too bad. I still know it's you under all that." His smile put her at ease. She motioned for him to come close and reached out to take his hand.

"Is Cindy okay?" he asked.

Allison smiled as wide as she could and nodded her head while tearing up. "Yes! Thank God! She has some bruised ribs and a concussion that they want to keep an eye on, but otherwise she's okay."

Ryan's relief was obvious. Allison squeezed his hand excitedly, then added, "But Randy is dead. They think some infection he had on his arm might have contributed to a fatal heart attack. Fortunately for us, it happened when it did. But before he died, he admitted to killing Mark. According to the police, what he told me checked out with how Mark really died." She paused, nervously patting his hand before continuing. "He snuck back into the house through my bathroom window and was planning to kill Cindy and me next."

Ryan squeezed her hand and pulled up a chair, then sat down. Allison was catching him up on the night's events when Daniel walked into the room.

Ryan and Daniel quickly shook hands and then Ryan insisted he take the chair next to Allison. Ryan took another chair and sat next to Daniel. Ryan casually winked at Allison as he sat back down in the chair a little farther away.

Allison again recapped the night's events and Ryan also offered additional information about their confrontation from the day before, as well as sharing his observations regarding the creek incident with Cindy. Feeling his cell phone vibrating in his pocket, Daniel excused himself from the room and took the call in the hall.

"I think he likes you," Ryan teased, as if they were

children on a playground.

Allison rolled her eyes, but didn't have time to respond before Daniel walked back into the room.

Daniel stood at the end of the bed. It was obvious he had news, so they remained quiet.

"We got the ballistics test back."

Allison and Ryan were locked at attention.

"It's a match to the gun recovered at your home."

Allison broke down crying. Daniel walked around to the other side of the bed and sat down, taking Allison's hand. "It's over. It's finally over," he said, gently squeezing her hand.

Ryan stayed a little longer before making the excuse that he wanted to go visit with Cindy. He clearly got the impression something was starting between Allison and Daniel and didn't want to be a third wheel.

After saying his goodbyes, Ryan stopped by Cindy's room, but she was asleep, so he decided to go home. Relieved they were ok, Ryan made his way back to the parking garage. He never liked Randy. And now knowing all that he did, he regretted not beating the shit out of him that night when he had the chance. Then he remembered the scratch on his arm. A twisted smile appeared on Ryan's face. "Karma's a bitch, asshole," he said out loud.

Chapter 27

A few days later, Ryan left work early and headed home for lunch and a nap. Gone was the rush of energy he'd been enjoying since the night of the concert. He was dragging and hoped some rest after lunch would do him good. Noticing activity at Allison's house, he walked over and knocked on the open front door.

"Knock, Knock, Knock," he announced, standing in the doorway. Allison and Cindy both emerged from the hall into the living room.

"Ryan!" Cindy shouted before running to him and engulfing him in a big hug.

Ryan scooped her up hugging her back. To Ryan, she was practically weightless.

Allison was still heavily bruised and moving slowly, but still beamed with excitement at seeing him.

They chatted for a few minutes, and Cindy caught Ryan up on how well the kittens were doing before returning to her room. Allison informed him that they were temporarily staying at her sister's place while she was out of town, then they planned to move to a condo her sister owned not far away. Ryan was familiar with the condo complex. He'd lived there himself before finding his current house. Allison also told him that they would not be returning to the neighborhood. Given all that had happened, as well as the year of bad memories, she thought it was best they start over fresh, just the two of them. When her sister offered the condo, she immediately took her up on it. Since Mark's passing, the upkeep of the house had proven difficult for one person. And going forward, she wanted as much free time with Cindy as possible. Ryan was sad to hear they would be leaving, but he also understood and volunteered himself and the band to help with the moving if she needed it.

"So, how are things with the detective?" Ryan asked. A sly smile curled his lips.

Allison blushed, then turned away, fidgeting with a pillow she quickly picked up off the couch. "We're taking it slow. I'm not jumping into anything right away."

Replacing the pillow back on the couch in a different orientation, she paused and then smiled back before adding, "But I have to say, Daniel has been very kind to me and Cindy."

Noticing how she lit up when talking about Daniel, Ryan raised his eyebrows a few times, teasing her. "Well, that's a good start."

They chatted a little longer before Allison returned to her bedroom to finish packing a few more items she wanted to take to her sister's.

After helping load some boxes into the car, Ryan popped in on Cindy to say goodbye. He knocked on her bedroom door before entering. Cindy was carefully packing a backpack with art supplies. As Ryan entered the room, he noticed several drawings on her desk. One looked strikingly like Tor.

"Hey, I know this guy. I let him in my house the night

of the show and he's been coming in every night since. As a matter of fact, he's probably over there somewhere right now. I put him out this morning before I left for work."

Cindy had her back to Ryan while she was packing. When she heard what he said she paused for a second, then subtly smiled. "He's been coming in to your house?" she asked.

"Yes. The night of the concert he showed up late and wanted inside. He reminded me of a cat that would sometimes join us when we rehearsed at the warehouse in Springfield. His name was Tor, so I've been calling this guy Tor as well." Ryan said holding the picture, impressed by the detail.

Still not facing Ryan, Cindy smiled. "Tor. I like that name," she said under her breath before turning around. "It must be your turn," she announced, looking directly at him.

Ryan didn't understand. Cocking his head, he clearly looked confused.

Cindy hurried to her bedroom door and looked out. Hearing her mom working in the room down the hall, she turned to Ryan and whispered, "Can you keep another secret?"

Ryan nodded and squatted down. Cindy quickly told him about the water moccasin, how the kittens arrived, and how Tor jumped up on the bench after Randy threw O, and how he scratched Randy, knocking him back. Ryan listened intently. For some reason he didn't feel she was making it up. But what she told him next left him speechless.

"When I was trying to escape through Biscuit's dog door, I saw Tor at the bottom of the steps. Randy pulled me back in and kicked and punched me. I remember running down the hall and him catching me. The next thing I remember is waking up next to the fireplace with a bright yellow-green glow coming from the hall. Then it went dark and a few seconds later Tor slowly approached me out of the darkness. I remember his cold wet nose touching mine! I do! And I remember feeling safe and that everything was going to be okay. Then the next thing I remember was the SWAT man."

Ryan was speechless. He had no doubts she believed what she was telling him.

"Did you tell anyone about the cat?" Ryan asked.

Cindy shook her head no.

"Why not?"

She shrugged her shoulders.

Ryan looked at the picture of Tor again.

"Maybe he's some kind of guardian angel."

Cindy smiled. "I think my daddy sent him to protect us. And now it's your turn," she said, looking at him with the sincerity and maturity of someone far older.

Ryan raised his eyebrows and bit his lip. Looking at the picture, his mind was clearly processing what she said.

Allison knocked on the bedroom door and entered the room. Seeing them both looking at the picture, she commented, "Isn't that a good drawing? Maybe she can come work for you one day?"

Ryan and Cindy both snapped-to in a moment of silent harmony and understanding. Cindy's secret would forever stay between them.

"Absolutely! I'd love to have her on my team," Ryan said, giving her a quick wink.

Ryan helped them load a few more things into Allison's car before saying goodbye. Allison strapped Cindy into the seat, then gave Ryan a very gentle hug. She was wearing a brace around her torso, making her movements awkward, yet she was managing.

Watching them back out of the driveway, Ryan waved. Replaying what Cindy said to him over in his head, he walked to the street, lost in thought as Allison's car disappeared around a bend in the road. Feeling something pressing against his shins, he looked down. Tor was there, rubbing excitedly against him.

"So, it's my turn, is it? I wonder what you have in store for me," Ryan said out loud. Tor's excitement was humorous. Ryan reached down and rubbed Tor's head and back.

"I still haven't had lunch yet. Are you hungry? Whatever it is you have planned for me, can it wait until after lunch? I'm starving. Then I feel like I could use a nap," Ryan joked as they walked up the driveway. Tor proudly trotted beside him with his tail straight up in the air.

RYAN AND TOR'S ADVENTURES
CONTINUE IN
TOR & THE IMMORTALS...

www.ingramcontent.com/pod-product-compliance
Lightning Source LLC
Chambersburg PA
CBHW070948120726
47910CB00004B/1157